T0196567

THE EDGE OF OBLITERATION

SIGYN PIWONKA

 www.trafford.com

North America & international
toll-free: 1 888 232 4444 (USA & Canada)
phone: 250 383 6864 ♦ fax: 812 355 4082

DEDICATION

I'd like to dedicate this novel to my boyfriend who has so kindly helped me mire through this original work with his sharp and poignant mind. I'd also like to acknowledge my father who read through my work even though it wasn't his cup of tea. Lastly, to my audience from fan fiction dot net, I hope that I won't disappoint you, and thank you for your continued support.

Just outside of Spartanburg, SC
October 16th, 2077, 0644h

Quinn Sondheim stopped his morning jog to catch his breath and take a quick swig of water from the light belt he wore. Sondheim was not young, but he was not old, either, and he had been faithful to maintain the discipline of running two miles each morning for the last fifteen years. He was now thirty-eight and wondered if he would ever have anything worthwhile to ever show from all of his hard work. True, he did own his own small pharmaceutical company based out of St. Petersburg, Florida by his own name, but Sondheim Incorporated still had a long way to go before they could truly achieve any of his higher ambitions.

Quinn hoped one day, as did many scientists of his ilk, to rid the world of the horrible disease of cancer. There were some doctors who had come up with several treatments and remedies to slow it down, perhaps, but no one could beset the effects from its mitigation and prevent it from ever invading the human body in the first place. Day after day, year after year, he and his fellow scientists squabbled over theories, hypotheses, and eventually experiments. But nothing worked, at least to his liking. The volunteers who had so generously donated themselves to their study rarely survived; naturally their families and loved ones desired revenge. If he didn't have such brilliant lawyers, Sondheim would have been out of business years ago.

Sondheim swatted away yet another swarm of mosquitoes and cursed to himself for neglecting to apply a liberal amount of bug spray onto himself before departing from his parents' house. Suddenly, he heard an electronic disturbance not very far away. It sounded like it was coming from not twenty yards behind him. He finished his water, slowly turned around, and removed a small rectangular object from his belt. Sondheim tapped three times onto the LCD screen and held the "magnafone" up.

"Magnafones" were like smart phones of older days in the twenty-first century but could do much more than send an email, surf the internet, take pictures, capture short movies, or play video games. When modified or 'modded' on the street, they could *also* serve as a pair of binoculars, disable complex electronics, detect infrared sensors as well as bugs, or even pick up the distortion fields that simple cloaking devices used. However, much to Sondheim's confusion, the magnafone saw absolutely nothing.

Again, he heard the noises but saw nothing with the magnafone or his naked eyes. A part of him told him not to go any closer, to just turn the hell around, and go back home. But that same boyish curiosity which led him to pursue a career in science drove his legs, though they were trembling, quite a bit closer. The noises were reminiscent of the 20th century film "The Wizard of Oz", in which Dorothy unmasked the high and mighty wizard as nothing more than a charlatan. He wondered if he would be able to do the same with this unseen conjurer. However, this one did not speak or ask him what he was doing here.

Sondheim took a huge breath to try and calm down his high blood pressure. Nowadays, before children were even born, their parents could introduce gene therapy into the baby before he or she fully developed as early as eight weeks. The therapy was still somewhat flawed, but no longer did parents have to worry about their children contracting some of their malignant hereditary traits, such as diabetes, myopia, or high blood pressure. However, Sondheim's parents did not opt for that treatment not only because of the steep price but also the fact that it was completely experimental at the time. The risk was too high for a hope and a prayer. So like many of his ancestors, Sondheim bested his genetic condition with exercise, a moderate diet, and medication.

He shoved the magnafone away into a sweaty back pocket of his shorts and hid behind the great trunk of an oak tree. The disturbance was now less than two yards away from him; suddenly, a large field of electronic energy, which he now assumed correctly were indeed cloaking fields, dispelled. A man in front of him with shockingly green eyes, platinum blonde hair, a soul patch, and an emerald overcoat turned away from what he had been working on and kicked the object. That cloaking field also dissipated to reveal a very large space craft.

"Toto, I don't think we're in Kansas anymore," he whispered to himself as his jaw dropped in awe.

"Who said that?" The man whirled around. "Show yourself or die by my hand right now." His hand withdrew some kind of pistol from his side.

Turn around and run away now, you fool, Quinn's father told him.

Quinn, if you know what's good for you, leave this place now, his mother urged him.

Sondheim ignored both of his parents' warnings, stepped away from the tree, and made himself visible to his perturbed host. He held up both of his hands in surrender and slowly walked towards the man. "Do not come any closer to me, human," the man ordered and held the pistol at Quinn. His voice was not pleasant, nor was the intonation completely homo sapient.

"Believe you me, I *won't*." Sondheim's eyes warily glanced at the weapon and then went back to the person in front of him. "So if you call me a human, you're obviously not one yourself. What are you?"

"The proper question is 'who are you', not 'what are you'?" The man corrected him and put away the gun once he realized that Sondheim was apparently unarmed. "You may call me Mercury."

"But—"

"I have selected it because your species used to worship this deity many years ago. He was a messenger for the gods, and you may think of me as such," Mercury candidly replied. "My people are in great need of your kind's assistance."

CHAPTER ONE

Zionastra Incorporated, San Francisco, CA
July 16th, 2079, 1820h

"Unacceptable. Either hire a competent lab associate or get off of your lazy hide and do some better work, Dr. Caroll!" Owen McGregor shouted over his magnafone to his subordinate. The technological device sat upon his enormous wooden desk.

"But sir—"

"I do not threaten; I file things electronically through my assistant," McGregor's volume lessened as he took a deep breath to calm himself down. "You have until the end of the week to get those nanites working properly, and that is all I will discuss with you for the moment. I expect your report then and no more excuses." He touched the skin just beneath his ear to end his call just as his phone began to ring yet again. "Yes?"

"Mr. McGregor, sir?" his assistant inquired. "Are you free?"

"From the ridiculous pain from my knee, no. But if you're asking if I can receive someone, send him or her in right away." McGregor collected a pitcher of water from the middle of his bureau and poured some water into a high ball glass.

"It's Armstrong, sir. He said that you wanted to see him at the end of the day."

"Send him in immediately and go home, Rachel."

"But Mr. McGregor . . ."

"That was not a request, Rachel. You're finished for the day. I may spend a great deal of time in this office, but I know all and can see all. Have a good weekend."

"I will, sir, thank you," came the reply.

Moments later, Nestor Armstrong strolled through the opaque sliding glass doors that led to McGregor's lavish office. This was the first time for him to actually come inside this place, even though he had been working as a security consultant for Zionastra for the past three years. He had just been promoted to second in charge to the company's head of security Vincent Honda, who kept a very tightly run department. Anyone who was caught taking outside bribes, calling in sick without a doctor's note, or sleeping on the job more than once was immediately dismissed upon the spot.

Armstrong kept himself in top shape, since he used to be a police officer with the San Francisco PD. He had an aquiline nose and a short but elongated strip of hair that went down the front of his chin for a beard. Not once did he let it grow out; he kept it neatly trimmed every single day. His milk chocolate eyes could stare down practically any suspect or perpetrator under his thumb but at the same time could also captivate nearly any woman he set them upon.

If there were any females in the area, several heads would turn or give him more than a once over; Armstrong was an extremely comely man. His hair was a much darker saturation than his eyes and his jaw was perfect. His upper teeth had a slight overbite, but it was not visible unless he smiled deeply. When he did smile or perhaps even smirk, there was always a playful hint that followed through with his eyes.

The muscles underneath the business suit he wore suggested that he was well-built but not overly beefy like some people in his department. He worked out when it was necessary to keep himself in shape, but he was not so vain as to spend so much time in the gym.

Armstrong had once applied to be a member of the US Coast Guard as well but failed the psychology test. Apparently, he was not the team player that the government wanted. But right now, the salary he made with Zionastra completely overshadowed some government employee to the tune of one whole decimal place. Honda liked him, too, and had taken him under his protective wing as soon as he started. He told Nestor that there was something special about him; he was not like his other colleagues. To that effect, Nestor offered a joke in reply, saying that he hoped not to be a regular cardboard cut out or the stereotypical security guard that Hollywood always had their hero bashing into the floor all too easily.

He whistled quietly to himself as he gawked at the opulent office. His eyes drank as much of it as he possibly could. The window behind the desk went from floor to ceiling; it was naturally tinted for privacy.

The bureau itself was fabricated from mahogany and an old fashioned but traditional golden inkwell was the only thing on his desk save the computer terminal with two large touch screen monitors. A decadent leather executive chair complete with circular brass inlays every two centimeters and two armrests that were made of teak faced the door along with two slightly more modest but nonetheless very comfortable client chairs. There were no picture frames upon this man's desk; he would not reveal any part of his personal life to anyone. *Damn, I figured that McGregor's office didn't have a place for sentimental objects*, Armstrong told himself. *That's fifty bucks Rodriguez owes me.*

"Good evening, Mr. Armstrong," McGregor called over to him, breaking him out of his inner thoughts. "Care to have a seat?"

"Sounds good to me," Armstrong replied casually and joined McGregor.

The boss had salt and pepper hair; his age was a bit difficult to nail down since so many people were now undergoing gene therapy. It was possible that McGregor could have been in his early fifties, but Armstrong would not make a bet on that.

"Sorry to spoil your weekend plans, Armstrong, but I'd like you to take a look at something that I've been working on." McGregor's perfunctory apology hit him in the face like a brick. He removed a bottle of pills from his desk, shook one out, popped it into his mouth, and washed the pill down with the water.

"That's all right, Mr. McGregor. Criminals love to perform on the weekends; their day jobs must suck out all their energy during the week."

"Don't you have some kind of date? Word is that you do get around." His employer gave him a smirk, and Armstrong stiffened up his posture. Honda did warn him that McGregor could be a vicious bastard and a snoop. However, he never actually involved himself with his employees' lives much other than one or two parties a year. Nor did he interfere with their personal lives, other than make the snide remark once in a while. "A new woman every other week, I hear."

Armstrong tried not to let his anger get the better of him; he kept a poker face. There was one time, though, when he was a police officer that he lost his patience. When Armstrong lost his temper, bad things happened very fast. The suspect they had caught was a known and convicted sexual predator as well as a child molester. He actually had the audacity to ask if Armstrong had any delicious looking children just like himself and licked his lips hungrily. At that point, Armstrong had just slapped the cuffs onto him and was about to take the man into the back of his cruiser. However, that was all Nestor could take. He slammed the perpetrator onto the trunk and broke the man's nose with his blackjack.

"I guess she can wait, then," Armstrong finally said with a shrug.

"Honda tells me that you're indispensable, and that you're exactly the sort of man I need for this job."

"Why not put Mr. Honda on this yourself?"

"Because he recommended *you*. And, he needs to keep up appearances." McGregor lifted up an old fashioned ink blotter and removed an electronic tablet much like the older 'iPads' from it. He slid the tablet across the desk over to Armstrong. "As you know, there is a heavy competition going on in between pharmaceutical and medical companies nowadays. And it's no secret that I despise Sondheim Incorporated with all my heart and soul. You've seen my public dismissal of their policies and entire manner of conducting business as I'm sure many people have."

That was an understatement. About two years ago, Sondheim Incorporated made a huge breakthrough in the medical world. They had the cure for cancer and were now literally making a killing. Their latest profit index suggested that the company was now worth several hundreds of trillions of dollars. McGregor openly stated to the press that although he could not prove it, Quinn Sondheim was cashing in on something cheap or dangerous to concoct this formula. In fact, he even called Sondheim a 'quack' right to his face during a humanitarian award ceremony in Tampa, Florida once. The media loved that story; it ran for a minimum of three days in the paper.

"So this medical technological babble means exactly what?" Armstrong wondered as his eyes read over the data.

"Look at the next log; it's a list of phone calls that Sondheim has been making with disposable cell phones over the past year. And it's *always* to the same number," McGregor stated and took a drink from his glass of water.

Phone calls could now be made with tiny little earpieces that appear to look like radio earpieces from older days. Most of the time, people kept them in their ears and never removed them; the technology could interact with a chip placed at the back of the neck, right near a person's spinal cord. You could literally think that you wanted to make a phone call, and as soon as your brain registered that it was a true desire, it sent an order to the phone as well as the number of the person you thought of. Or if you scanned a new number into your eyes with your magnafone, it could call that as well. If you were receiving a phone call, your brain would send three tiny little charges to your fingers or toes, depending on your own preferences.

Criminals who did not want to be tracked did not use their implants to make phone calls; they used disposable cell phones, aka "burners" and destroyed them immediately after each use. The signals could still be traced, but unfortunately since the phones were so small and delicate, they could be destroyed all too quickly and easily. "So you want to take him down," Armstrong offered, to which McGregor agreed with a nod.

"More or less."

Or perhaps McGregor wanted the cure for himself. Zionastra was doing relatively well on the medical science market but paled in comparison to Sondheim Incorporated.

"What do you need me to do, sir?"

"I have an inside source coming from within Sondheim Incorporated itself. She suspects that something isn't quite right with them but cannot get any solid evidence without some help." He paused to take another drink of water, and Armstrong leaned forward in his chair with interest. "She's got the expendable cell phone with her now and has promised to meet you in an hour's time. You've got two options that she's aware of: you can go in the front door pretending to have a business meeting with her or sneak in by infiltrating the neighboring building and finding some kind of way across it. How you do it is completely up to you, Armstrong."

"You're letting me make the choice?"

"Just let me know so that I can call my chopper pilot. I do happen to have him waiting on the line, by the way."

"Do you have a name of the contact and a physical description?"

"Yes and no. I have a name, and that's it. Oh, and . . . here's another . . . mmm . . . snag to this assignment, Armstrong."

"Yes?"

"You shouldn't kill anyone. If you do, things could become, shall we say . . . messy?"

"Blood does leave nasty stains everywhere," Armstrong smirked.

"Her name is Penelope Liszt and like you, she's second in charge to Hank Wooster, the head of Sondheim Incorporated's security. Now, I can smooth things over with the police somewhat, but start to rack up the lobby with dead bodies, and . . .—" McGregor lifted up a finger and waved it back and forth as if he were scolding a mere child and not an adult. "You can kiss your Christmas bonus goodbye."

"Remember that I used to be a cop, too, for this city, even?"

"Yes, Mr. Honda did mention that. Well, even so, I imagine that you would not like to have to confront any of your former colleagues, would you, now?"

Armstrong started to open his mouth to retort a wisecrack but then decided to prudently shut it and slid the electronic tablet back over to McGregor. "An hour from now, you say?"

"Yes. So will you need that helicopter lift or not?" McGregor demanded.

Armstrong considered his options and rolled his neck around as he thought. He noticed his boss' fingers start to tap impatiently upon the ink blotter and after another thirty seconds, he shook his head 'no'. "I'll take my bike over there and walk in the front door. Thank you, though, sir."

"Make sure you visit Nathan Falk on your way out before you depart for Sondheim Inc. He's staying an extra half an hour for you and you alone, Armstrong." McGregor's eyes narrowed. "And I'm paying him overtime already."

"I'll be on my merry way, then. Hope your leg feels better." The ex-cop arose from his seat.

"Now that my nervous system down there has been fully nullified, I'll be fine for the next four hours or so. I look forward to meeting this woman upon your return. Don't be surprised if something changes during this little task. Two companies that are arch rivals in the medical technological field can have . . . mmm . . . unpleasant clashes."

"I'm sure," Armstrong responded dryly and left the office. *I've had more than enough of that man for one day. I certainly hope that plans will change.*

Zionastra Armory and Laboratory
July 16th, 2079, 1856h

The Zionastra armory was run by Nathan Falk, a technological genius from Ireland. He'd never actually say where, though, as Armstrong had asked him several times. He was stout and relatively short in height like so many of his ancestors; he even had real strawberry blonde hair with blue eyes. The first time that he and Armstrong met, Armstrong naturally tossed out his best Irish brogue and asked Falk if he had any Lucky Charms. He was swiftly rewarded with a lively punch to his jaw.

Their relationship had improved over time slowly; that was two years ago. Now Falk and Armstrong were finally on a friendly first name basis, though sometimes Falk still called Nestor by his surname on occasion.

His fellow assistants scurried about like rabbits; they each feared both their immediate supervisor as well as Armstrong.

As Armstrong strolled out of the elevator, their pace quickened. He walked right over to one of their stations, gave the man a rogue smile, and was just about to put his finger onto the piece of technology when the man shook his head 'no'. "Please don't touch that, sir."

"Is it going to shock me?" Armstrong wondered.

"Not upon immediate contact, no. But if you touch something else afterward . . ." The assistant turned to face him and made a slashing gesture across his throat.

"Nice to know that you're all working so fervently upon something that's so devastating. Have you put that into a weapon yet?"

"That will come in time," Nathan's light accent warmed him, and Armstrong turned to his left. "Mr. McGregor told me what I need to know about your mission. Planning on going behind enemy lines, eh?"

Armstrong shrugged with a sheepish grin. "I've done it before when I went undercover as a cop. Thankfully, I won't have to spend much time in there. We already have an infiltrator."

Falk led him over to a table and placed a small automatic pistol into his hands. "This looks just like your standard 9mm Smith and Wesson M&P 9. However," he said and released the clip magazine to let Nestor gaze upon the rounds.

"These don't look like rubber, bean bag, or plastic slugs." He brought the clip up closer to his eyes for an inspection. "What the hell—"

"Tranquilizer bullets, naturally. They look just like regular slugs, except," Falk removed one of them from the magazine, "back here on the casing is a yellow dot."

"So I probably couldn't attach a silencer to this puppy even if I wanted to, right?"

"Since the gun is actually firing compressed air at the same velocity of a regular bullet, it will be three times as soft in decibels, so that won't be necessary, Armstrong." Falk shook his head 'no'. "One of these is the equivalent to putting down a bear. Or perhaps just a small one at that. I wouldn't go chasing after any grizzly or kodiak bears with it if I were you."

"I like a good hunt like the next man," Armstrong joked.

"And this beauty," Falk said as he introduced his colleague to the next firearm with a finger, "is what I like to call the 'Luke'."

"What? Looks like your everyday assault rifle to me, a bit like the good old Barrett REC7," Nestor picked the gun up and tested its balance in his hands.

"Surely it does, my friend, by all outward appearances. The magazine, though, does not carry slugs. Each cartridge carries charges of sound waves; they leave the muzzle at 3.6k FPS. You will not need to reload; the weapon will recharge itself in three seconds' time."

"So it'll knock someone off of their feet to the ground? Make 'em unconscious?"

"Exactly; the tested distance was about two hundred meters. Any farther away than that, and the effect will lessen," Falk placed his hands upon his hips. "But be careful with the 'Luke'. Sending several of these charges into a person can actually be quite deadly, and I think McGregor wants to avoid that as much as possible."

"So that's the maximum distance, but what's the minimum? Could I actually kill a person with this thing if it's too close to someone?" Armstrong closed an eye and activated the laser targeting scope on the barrel to look down it.

"That is possible. In fact, it's probably deadly from the distance we're standing apart right now," Falk stated and pointed towards the both of them. "So if you don't mind, please be careful with Luke."

"Why the hell do you call it a Luke?"

"I'll let you translate it by yourself one day, but understand that it comes from a language I don't speak fluently."

Armstrong rolled his eyes. "Well, *that* narrows it down, thank you, Falk."

"So, speaking of using your head, would you like to use goggles or a helmet this evening?"

"Ooh, I have a choice in the matter today?"

"That you do, Mr. Armstrong, only because I'm feeling quite generous."

"Goggles, I guess. I'll already be wearing a motorcycle helmet on my way over. I might as well complete the set."

"And please do remember to try to take cover when your shields go down, Armstrong. That protective nano suit alone cost this company five million dollars."

An assistant came over to them, placed the goggles into Falk's hand, and waived to him. "Good night, Mr. Falk, see you in the morning, sir. And please try not to break all of our equipment, Mr. Armstrong, if you can." He practically ran out the door.

"No promises," Armstrong called to him with a hand over his mouth to amplify his voice. "Any more toys, Nathan?" he turned to the Irishman and put the luke back onto the table in front of him.

"Indeed." Falk gathered some triangular shaped objects about the size of a quarter pound hamburger patty and let Armstrong feel one in his hand.

"Smoke bombs and incendiaries? Is it my birthday today?"

"Now I *really* wonder if your mum didn't drop you on your head when you were just a tot, Armstrong." He folded his arms across his chest. "Please again, try to only use the whitey blarneys for distractions and not to kill anyone."

"Blarneys?" Armstrong inquired with an amused tone. "What's wrong with calling them 'white petes'?"

"Well, these have got an extra edge to the phosphorus ones you're familiar with. Not only will this burn your eyes and skin out but will also send out nasty little nanite buggers that'll burrow into your flesh and make you itch like crazy for the next six hours. I'm quite proud of 'em."

"So when was your birthday again, Nathan?" Nestor impulsively scratched his forearm.

"Gone and passed for the year, man. Don't try to remind me how old I am compared to you. Rubbing salt into the wound ain't advisable." Falk's eyebrows both arose irritably.

"It wasn't my intention." Armstrong held up his hands in defense. "I plead the fifth."

"Humph. Any other questions?"

"How many can I take with me?" he grinned devilishly.

Falk simply stared his younger friend down and shook his head. "You know, there was a sweet . . . ah, never mind. You're not interested in that rot."

"If it's a secret about your dark and mysterious past, now I *have* to know."

"You watch too many movies, Nestor."

Armstrong walked over to a locker and started to work upon the combination on the LCD's three tumblers. "Spill it or I'll make all of your lackeys squeal like a little girl."

"Well since one of them already *is* a woman, that's a moot point, Nestor," Falk groused and put both of his hands onto his hips. "And she's immune to your charms."

"Oh yeah," Armstrong said with a chuckle. He had once tried and miserably failed to talk Inga Bergmann into going to dinner with him. She wiggled her left ring finger upon his request, which had made his cheeks redden with utter embarrassment. "I doubt she'd ever leave her husband for me, even though I am better looking."

"Maybe he's got some other talents that you just don't know about because Inga's a lady and doesn't discuss 'em in the workplace. Ah, well, I was just remembering the name of a sweet woman there at Sondheim . . . Lily? Yes, that's right. Lily Kaufmann." His face darkened when he remembered what had occurred between them.

Armstrong opened the locker and began to disrobe his business suit. "What? What happened to her?"

"It's nothing," Nathan waived his hand dismissively in thin air.

"Does she still work there? Is she your age?"

"I'll speak of her no more, not tonight anyhow, while I'm still sober. Anyhow, lock up when you're finished, lad. See you on Monday."

"Wait a second." Falk was about to head towards the exit when Armstrong came over to him still partially undressed. "What if something goes wrong with my equipment? I've got you on speed dial, can't I—"

"You think I haven't tested any of this?!" he roared. "I spend 80% of my life in here, and now that I want one day or so of peace to myself—"

"You said Monday. That's three days from now."

"True, but I'm going to get at least one quote emergency call from one of my associates here because he or she screwed something the hell up. I just know it. Now get on with your bloody mission and do what you have to do!" With that, Falk stormed out of the armory.

"Is he always that angry when he leaves work?" Armstrong questioned the last scientist, who nodded a 'yes'.

"Every single damn day. You just learn to tune him out," he replied. The scientist studied the tattoo that was upon Armstrong's right shoulder upon his naked back. "I was thinking about getting one of those one day. That's a phoenix, right? Are those Chinese characters underneath it; what do they mean?"

"It's the creature's name. They call it a fenghuang and consider it to be a composite of all birds." Armstrong stepped into his navy blue polymer-nano suit, which he nicknamed 'Spidey' after the Amazing Spiderman. The suit was made with nanotechnology that was patented only to Zionastra, to Nathan Falk, particularly. The material was ten times lighter than kevlar, but it had the same amount of protection. It almost resembled a wet suit that surfers wore.

"Have you ever been there, to China, I mean?"

"Not yet."

"Can I ask you something, Mr. Armstrong?"

"Sure." Nestor journeyed over to the table to start loading the grenades as well as some spare ammunition into his backpack.

"Why do you wear an overcoat like that?" He gestured to the coat hanging upon the locker's door.

Armstrong chortled and gave the assistant a large smile. "Style."

The scientist's forehead wrinkled with confusion, and he left soon thereafter.

The real reason was to partially cover up the fact that he was carrying so much firepower.

CHAPTER TWO

Sondheim Incorporated, San Francisco, CA July 16th, 2079, 1928h

The ride over to the huge skyscraper of Sondheim Incorporated was uneventful, and Armstrong parked the motorcycle about three blocks away from it in an alley. He glanced upon his old fashioned wrist watch, confidently strolled up the concrete staircase to the automated doors, and walked through them in a breeze. *Sundown isn't for at least another hour. I hope that this won't be too hard.*

"How can I help you?" a security officer with the name 'Abe' stitched along the left side of his uniform inquired with a wary tone. He sat perched upon a pneumatic stool that was surrounded by several touch screen monitors probably showing only a few different camera angles. The real monitoring system was located elsewhere, likely in the heart of the building and three times as large with two guards' eyes upon it at all times.

Armstrong's eyes scoured the bureau and took notice of a digital frame that showed a woman holding one child and two others that stood on either side of her with their arms crossed against their chests with unhappy expressions. "Nice family. Neither of mine would stand still for their photo either. At least you got them to *look* at the camera," Armstrong lied.

A beam came across Abe's lips, and his voice became quite a bit more friendly. "Yeah, that in itself was a miracle. Where would you like to go, sir?"

"I've got an appointment to see Specialist Penelope Liszt. Could you please tell me where I can find her office?"

The sentry's eyes left Armstrong's and went down to the computer terminal in front of him, no doubt to read an instant message. He then glanced upward back up to Nestor and continued to smile. "You'll find it on the fourth floor. Just take one of the elevators right over there," he signaled his thumb behind himself," and the office is at the end of the hallway to your left. I just sent her a message; she's expecting you now, sir."

"Thank you, Abe." Armstrong gave him a perfunctory smile and bowed his head slightly forward.

"You're welcome, sir."

As he waited for the elevator to take him to his destination, Armstrong ran over what just happened in his mind. He was relatively okay with people, but something seemed a bit off with that conversation. The security officer was still too friendly. *Nothing's ever this easy. I'd better prepare for a surprise greeting.*

The elevator arrived upon the fourth floor, and Armstrong cautiously stepped out. There were four guards in the area, but none of them appeared to be hostile. He casually journeyed down the corridor and stopped at the last door on the left. Before going inside, he took a glance around the corner. *This doesn't smell right.*

As he suspected, each of them now began to head in his direction. *Yep. I thought so. Guess that guy at the front desk thought I had the word 'stupid' plastered across my forehead.*

Nestor jogged into the open office, withdrew the luke from his backpack, and unfolded it. His eyes quickly surveyed the office for cover, and he found a very suitable hiding spot from behind a metallic desk. The footsteps that had been walking down the hallway quickened; he had little time left. He also threw over a rectangular table to face the door that had previously been full of office supplies and data tablets for some extra cover. It would do as a fast shelter to roll over to when he needed to make a dash for the office's one and only exit.

Armstrong double checked that the luke's safety was off as well as the trigger guard and hugged himself behind the desk first. *I wonder if they're gonna use real live rounds or stun guns. Honda normally makes us use those damned zapper guns. Thank God they can actually fire electron fields now without those leads any more. Don't know how those law enforcement officers used to make do with those clumsy things in earlier years.*

His question was answered in no time when the guards opened fire and bullets shattered the glass behind him as well as began to riddle the desk. *Now that's smart. They can't see me and immediately open fire. Oh well.*

He waited until the automated gunfire stopped, leaned out, and let off a few rounds from the luke. His arm reminded him of the luke's true power. "Whew. That's got some recoil," he mused. "Too bad I didn't have time to practice with you before I left."

He made contact with three of the men; the other intelligently used the table that Armstrong had flipped over previously for cover. The blasts did as Falk promised; the sentries appeared to not only be off their feet but unconscious as well. But unfortunately, the one left in the room had just reloaded his semi-automatic pistol, and he was now waiting for Armstrong to make a move. "I'm glad that one of you has brains," Armstrong called out, hoping to distract the guard. "What kind of gun is that, a Beretta?"

The man did not take the bait but rather cocked the pistol.

"How about an H&K? Germans make damned good firearms."

"Can't talk right now," the guard finally responded into his radio.

That was all Armstrong needed. He vaulted himself over the bureau, ran towards his opponent, and surprised him with a shot in the chest. The guard slumped onto the floor, and Nestor winced as he just now remembered what Falk had warned him about. He touched the man's cheek and felt for a pulse upon his neck; there was none. "Shit. Guess I'd better put this away for now."

Armstrong secured the luke to the gun rack upon his backpack and pulled the tranquilizer pistol out from its holster upon his hip. He bent down to examine one of the unconscious guards and pulled the earpiece out of his ear. He next retrieved his own personal magnafone from his weapon belt, rolled the man over, and scanned the magnafone upon the guard's implant to retrieve the radio frequency that they were currently using.

"Gotcha." Moments later, he lifted the magnafone up to his eyes and 'read' the data. His brain processed it and sent the information to the implant. Seconds later, he heard the radio communication chatter going through his head.

"We've got a visitor on floor number four here. None of the team up there is currently responding to my hails," an officer stated. "They're probably dead. Live rounds, zappers, or beanbags, ma'am?"

"Definitely do *not* use live rounds. Dead bodies mean the police," a female voice responded with a foreign inflection. *She is certainly not from the U.S.*, Armstrong figured. "Try not to take the intruder out. I'd like the person conscious when you bring him or her in."

Ah, she's resourceful. She knows I'm coming but doesn't want to tip anyone else off. Good. Maybe she'd fire those morons who shot first instead of asking questions.

Armstrong put his magnafone away, arose, and decided to take the stairs to his next destination. He sighed and hoped that Liszt's office wasn't too far away. As much as he liked a good workout, he also liked to get things done quickly so that he could move onto the next task or perhaps even some time off for himself. *I never understand type A people. They're too high-strung.*

"We're approaching the fourth floor now from the elevator, although he's probably moved on by now," the same guard reported.

"Don't take any chances. I still want to know what happened to our people," Penelope responded calmly.

Good, she's buying me time. Her voice reminds me of . . . oh . . . well, I don't care. It's kind of sexy and low; now I'm kind of hoping that she's no butch.

"Will you be needing extra back-up, ma'am?"

"I'll be fine here on the second floor for now."

Damn. Maybe they won't search the stairs.

Armstrong wasted no more time; he hurried down the steps and unfortunately ran into some traffic in between the second and third floors. "He's in the stairwells in between levels two and three! Backup!" one guard yelled just as Armstrong swept him off of his feet with a low kick. He then hunched over the man before he could get back up and sneaked an arm around his throat. Armstrong squeezed his throat just enough so that the guard lost consciousness and then got back up.

He ran inside the door marked '2' and was greeted by two officers. "Oh, hello!" he announced with a cavalier grin and promptly fired his tranquilizer gun into both of their necks. Both of them plopped onto the floor, and Armstrong dragged their bodies over to the door. He lay one partially on top of the other so that anyone who hurried through that door would probably trip over them.

When he turned back around and arose, at least four guards had their pistols and assault rifles pointed at him. He sighed, dropped his tranquilizer gun onto the ground, and wrapped both of his hands around the back of his head to surrender. "Is there any chance that I could get that back before I leave? It's worth a bunch of money."

"Then it'll fetch quite a bit on eBay or Craig's List," that same female voice he heard on the radio told him in his ear. Armstrong's eyes searched the corridor for her but then remembered that he was wearing one of their earpieces. "Yes, I know that you've taken one of our radios. Do come in, Mr. Armstrong."

"Want us to take his equipment, ma'am?" a sentry questioned Liszt.

"I'll do that myself in here. Please show him the way."

"You heard the boss. Move it," the same guard ordered Armstrong with a gesture using his pistol. He then jabbed it into Armstrong's lower back when he started to dawdle.

"Remind me to thank her for your extra kind hospitality," Armstrong jeered. "You're alive and unharmed for the most part."

"So when does your shift end?"

"In about an hour."

"So what's the rush? Got a hot date?"

"You're awfully chatty for some kind of assassin." The officer opened the door for Armstrong, who spun around and gave him a wink. "Need us for anything, Miss Liszt?"

The woman in front of him was dressed in a sharp charcoal gray business pants suit. She had milk chocolate skin the same hue as Armstrong's eyes, and she had blonde highlights in her brown hair as well as deep sorrel eyes. Liszt arose from her seat with a large zip tie, signaled him to put his hands down, and secured them behind his back. "No, Simon. Tell everyone else to stand down but to be alert, just in case," she announced with a proud and confident air. She retrieved her own receiver from her ear.

"As you say, ma'am," Simon stated with a salute and closed the door.

Liszt traveled back over to Armstrong. "Left or right?"

"Sorry?"

She sighed and rolled her eyes over having to explain herself. "Do you hear better out of your left or right ear?"

"I'm not sure. Six months ago, they told me that I had way too much wax in my left one, but—"

She huffed impatiently, stuck two fingers into his right ear, and pulled out the earpiece. "Everyone, mute your radios for a second, I'm going to destroy something," she commanded. Without waiting for any sort of confirmation, she dropped both radios onto the floor, and smashed her booted heel onto them.

"Now what the hell good did that do? Am I not the one who's supposed to help you get out of here?" Armstrong growled. "And what's with the wrist binding, anyhow?"

"I've got a spare in my desk. And I've got to keep up appearances, just in case my boss decides to drop in on us."

"Penelope Liszt, I presume? I'd shake hands with you, but I'm afraid that that's a bit impossible right now."

"Yes, well, please have a seat." She gestured to one of the soft cushioned client chairs in front of her desk. He studied her as she glided herself around the desk and opened an electronically sealed combination lock to access a drawer.

"Think I'll stand."

"Suit yourself."

"So . . . this is a bit unorthodox. Is this how you usually go about having somebody brought up here for a conference? I'd hate to see what you'd have done to a client meeting you for lunch or a drink," Armstrong joked as he approached her bureau.

"Honda didn't say you had a sense of humor." Liszt raised up an irked eyebrow.

"It releases tension." He shrugged and stood at ease. "So you apparently know some things about me, but I don't know anything about you, other than the fact that you like to tie a man down."

"Has it occurred to you that women don't like men who flirt?"

"No; I've heard just the opposite, actually. Anyway, deflecting my question with another is the highest form of flattery."

At least it is to me. You don't want to talk about it because it makes you uneasy. When she finally got into the drawer, she pulled out a plastic petri dish.

"So, is that what I think it is?" Armstrong demanded.

"Yes. But I want to know what your boss' goals are before I let him take a glance at this or listen to any of the conversations," Liszt informed him.

"You'll have to ask him that yourself; I'm not sure. What I'm here to do is to make sure that you get there safely. And . . . you've got actual audio?"

"So he didn't tell you." Her eyes narrowed. "Interesting."

"I know what I need to know; sometimes asking questions that deal with things outside the assignment's parameters can be detrimental and lead to trouble," Armstrong said as he tilted his neck from side to side, getting out the kinks that had settled there.

"Or doing so can open up your eyes about what kind of a person you truly work for," Liszt responded gently. "I don't trust either of you very much yet." Her index finger slid quickly across an electronic tablet now.

"No kidding. So what else can you tell me about what Mr. Sondheim has been up to?"

"Humph. I thought you said that you knew everything that you wanted to know."

"Touché." His eyes left her hands and went elsewhere. They actually went somewhere very unprofessional, and about fifteen seconds later, she lifted her head up to give him a reticent scolding. "So now that our date's over, when should we leave?"

"I believe that that last area you were gaping at constitutes as a second date, Mr. Armstrong, not a first." She paused to give one last look at the tablet, took out a switchblade, and came towards him.

He swallowed a lump the size of a golf ball down his throat as she pressed the little switch upon the knife's hilt and smoothly cut the zip-tie that was binding his wrists together behind his back. "Where are you from? That's not a British accent."

"It isn't; I'm originally from Cape Town, South Africa. Now let's move along." Liszt collected the petri dish, put it into a pocket, and removed a Sig Sauer P220 Diamond Plate from an arm holster.

"What were you doing?"

"Uploading a virus into the company's electronic security measures. It should work as soon as we walk outside of this office." She inserted another radio earpiece into her canal.

Armstrong rotated his wrists around to get some circulation flowing back into them and glanced at her. "Just so you know, killing wasn't part of my mission protocol. Would you really gun down all of these people who used to call you boss and look up to you?"

"Wooster was the one who ordered those people on the fourth floor to shoot at you with live rounds; I had previously told them to use beanbag slugs or zappers. He'll probably do it again once the virus gets released into the system. Come on, we're wasting time here."

"Yes, ma'am," he mocked her with the same tone that Simon had used. She gave him a spiteful glare as he withdrew the luke assault rifle from his backpack. "Good to go now. After you."

Once they arrived outside, Armstrong turned the gun the opposite way round and used his rifle butt this time to knock the sentry out. Unfortunately, Liszt chose to shoot the guard who was closest to her. "Was I speaking a foreign tongue when I said that we should minimize casualties?" he groused.

"That was an order given to *you* by your superior and not to me," she snapped back coldly.

"Yeah, well I was also trying to avoid *that*," he pointed to the two officers who now sprinted down the hallway towards them.

"Point taken." Before either of the men could stop and fire their guns, she took a careful aim and fired several bullets into each.

"Then I hope you brought plenty of spare .45 clips with you, 'cause I sure don't have any, Dirty Harriet," Armstrong retrieved his tranquilizer pistol from the floor where he'd previously dropped it and secured it to his hip holster once more.

"So your company's also got an armory that modifies weapons? What exactly do you think that says about your employer?" Liszt wondered as they came to the end of the hall, and she pushed the lift's call button.

"It says that they value human life. Isn't that going to take a while to get here? I don't like waiting around while they can still—"

"Relax, Mr. Confidence. They're scattered and re-grouping on the stairs." She signaled his attention to the radio chatter going on in her ear. "They'll probably still trip over those two bodies you left by the doorway there."

"So they're not using the elevator?" Armstrong gave her an odd look. "Why's that?"

"Because it doesn't go down to the garage. Only the stairwells do," she shook her head 'no'.

"We don't need to go down there. I parked my bike a couple of blocks away." The elevator came, and they both stepped inside. She nearly hesitated before pressing the "G" button, so he did so himself. "Problems?"

"I'm not very fond of . . . well . . .—"

"You'd rather fight your way through a couple of dozen security guards to get to your car? Really? And people tell me that *I've* got a death wish," he said as he rolled his eyes.

"I'd really . . . rather not . . . ride on a . . ." Her speech genuinely slowed down as her eyes made contact with the floor. "On a . . . motorcycle."

"Why's that?"

"They just . . . make me . . . uncomfortable," she stammered.

"Damnit, woman, this doesn't make things any easier. This evidence had better be worth it," he grunted and pressed the "1" button instead.

"Thank you," was all she said in response.

The rest of the ride was in silence as they prepared themselves for the inevitable assault that waited for them upon the ground floor. No one was there, though, which meant exactly what both of them already knew. The attack was going to be waiting for them on the stairwell.

"What're they preparing for now?" he queried.

"Precisely what I feared. The door's been rigged with a proximity mine. If either of us come within three feet of it . . ." she snapped her fingers. "Sadly, I can't disable it with my magnafone; that app didn't come with my modifications."

"Boom. Okay. What about going through the garage entrance?"

"That could work. Did you bring any distractions with you?"

He gave her a lopsided grin. "I've got one standing right next to me."

She actually gave him half a smile. "I meant to ask you if you brought any grenades with you."

"That I did; shall we head outside and sneak around the back? Or is the entrance in the alley to the western part of the building? At least, that's what I thought I saw as I was walking towards this place."

"Honda said that you used to be a policeman. Indeed, that is true. Let's be on our way, then," Liszt declared.

Without another second to spare, they both bolted out the Sondheim Incorporated edifice and jogged around the corner down the alley. "Damn. I think they might be onto us," she told him after they both hugged the brick wall. "Want to provide us some suppressing fire while I search for the bombs in your knapsack?"

"So how long have you been in the security business again?" He turned his head towards her to make this remark.

"Well, I'd offer to do so, but I'm afraid that I wouldn't be able to properly fire that thing without some practice," she admitted, gestured to the luke, and holstered her pistol.

"All right." Armstrong devoted his full attention to the security forces that were now congregating towards them. He spun himself around so that not only was he protected by the wall but she by him. Nestor was about to start firing the gun until she tapped him on the shoulder with the slight clearing of her throat.

"Can't reach," was all she said, and he bent down upon one knee.

One second later, the luke began to shoot out its wide range of sound waves upon the enemy. She crouched with him and unzipped the knapsack. "Hmm, such a curious assortment you've got here. Which ones do what?"

"Blue colors are smoke; the orange ones are what my armorer calls 'white blarneys'," he yelled above the gunfire.

"What?"

He scooted himself back into cover to avoid hostile bullets, and she followed his body's movements swiftly. "Phosphorous explosives with a bit more kick."

"Why not white?" She took out two of each and zipped the pack back up.

"Dunno; you can ask him that if you meet him."

"Perhaps I will. Do I need to arm this somehow?" Liszt asked as she examined the grenades.

"They should explode upon impact. That's one great thing about Falk; he always remains consistent with his triggers." Armstrong turned to shoot the luke again.

"Right. What's the blast radius?"

"Ten feet and probably . . ." he stopped briefly to lick a finger and hold it up to gauge the speed of the wind. "Will probably take about six seconds to dissipate. Don't ask me about the smoke bombs, though. I have no clue."

"Only one way to find out, then." She didn't wait for him to finish firing; she lobbed the grenade blindly towards the tangos.

There was a break in the fire as well as a lot of cries of pain from the enemies, so the white blarney must have done quite a bit of damage. Liszt removed her magnafone from her pocket and activated it to scan for bodies through the white cloud. "Looks clear for now. Want me to toss out the smoke bomb as well as we make a break for it?"

"Couldn't hurt," he shrugged.

She tossed the other grenade in front of them; when the smoke began to fill the area, he followed her lead as they sprinted towards the cars. "Uh-oh. Throw the other smoke grenade, Liszt," Armstrong told her and took a quick backward glance.

"Are you sure?"

"*Now*." His voice was so authoritative that she did not hesitate and immediately obeyed him. Smoke once again obscured the security officers from being able to locate their position. He fired the luke aimlessly so that they'd keep their distance, and he eventually caught up to her.

They finally came to her car; she started the engine with her magnafone and unlocked the doors. "Do you ever wonder if we'll have cars that fly someday?" Armstrong wondered. He watched in complete amazement as she threw the car into reverse, smoothly shifted gears, and made a total one-eighty all in less than five seconds.

"And interfere with all the airplanes, choppers, and jets that are already up in the sky? I can see how well *that* plan would work out," she replied dryly. "Oh, bollocks. Wooster's one tenacious and determined bastard. That virus I sent should only work for about twenty-four hours in the system. He must now be harboring some sort of grudge against me."

"What's wrong? Oh, never mind." He cut his question short after he realized that an SUV was now chasing them. "I don't suppose that I should have to tell you to step on it, should I?"

"If you can drive faster around a garage any better, then I suggest we switch places, Armstrong," she quipped and whipped the car around a corner.

A large crack in the back windshield quickly put an end to their disagreement from a bullet, and he slammed his fist into the button on his door. The interior lights of the car now turned on, and she gave him a furious glare. "What're you trying to do?"

"Open the damn window, of course," he spat.

"Why didn't you ask, you chop?!" Liszt groaned and activated a switch on her steering wheel as they came to the garage's entrance. "Hang on, don't try anything yet. I'm gonna floor it and make a ninety around the corner to see if I can shake them."

Two more shots successfully penetrated the windshield, and the glass now shattered inside the car as well as outside of it. True to her word, Liszt did as she promised, but the SUV kept up with her.

"You know where you're going, right?" Armstrong asked her.

"Naturally. We've only got to get to the interstate. They wouldn't dare follow us there because of the traffic cams. In fact, there are some right along this street."

"Would the cameras even be able to get a decent shot of their plates at the current speed we're making?" Before she could answer him, he leaned out of the window and began to fire the luke at the pursuing SUV.

"Making any impacts?" Her eyes went to the rear view mirror to double check his honesty.

"None whatsoever." He lithely sneaked himself back inside, threw the rifle into the back seat, and wiggled himself out of the backpack.

She chose to remain silent as her eyes now focused on the road and careened their little sedan around another corner flawlessly again.

I'll say one thing about her; at least she can drive, he thought as he dug into the satchel for another grenade.

The SUV swerved to nearly miss a semi-truck in the oncoming lane as it almost did not make the turn around the corner. He pulled out the smoke grenade, flicked a toggle switch, held it outside to let it catch the wind, and finally jettisoned the object behind them. Their pursuant tried to veer off to the other side of the road but this time collided head-on with another SUV just like it.

"Lekker," she muttered to herself as she watched the cars merge into one giant wreck and began to slow down to a legal speed. "Very nice."

"Do you think that they'll send another vehicle after us?"

"No. I'd keep this, but . . ." Liszt murmured, reached into her ear, and tossed the radio onto the sidewalk.

"They'd be able to triangulate our position. What about your magnafone?"

She brought the car to a full stop for a red light and sighed. "I just bought a new one last week, too."

"Fork it over, Dirty Harriet. We can get you another one." Armstrong's fingers shot over toward her chest as he kept an eye on the road; she winced as they came so close towards her breasts.

"Watch it."

"Sorry," he said with a shrug. *For once, my eyes weren't watching my hands.*

"Fine. I want the exact same model and features that came with this one." Liszt dug into a suit coat pocket and placed the magnafone into his palm. He next proceeded to drop it out of the window. "And ekse, Mr. Armstrong, why do you keep calling me Dirty Harriet?" She made a left turn at the light and rolled the car's windows up as they came up the ramp to the interstate. "Air conditioning to forty percent. Headlights to nighttime intensity," she commanded the car's internal computer system in a flat voice.

"Let's make a deal," Armstrong began.

"I'm open for a discussion, not a transaction."

"It's only verbal, so relax, Dirty Harriet."

"There's that bloody nickname again." This time, she did not huff or roll her eyes when he said it; he swore that he saw another smile creep onto her face, though. It was difficult to see her expressions since the sun had gone down now.

"Yes. I'll tell you what it means . . . over a mutually shared cup of coffee."

"I suppose you're asking me out on a date."

"Look at it however you'd like, Ms. Liszt. Just remember, you're the one who called it that first and not me." He held up a finger.

"Hmm . . . just remember, Mr. Armstrong . . . two can play at emotional blackmail." That was her last comment for the remainder of their drive.

Well, well, well. So much for her dislike for flirting. Now, what was the name of that woman I was supposed to meet at the Black Horse London Pub? His eyes once again wandered into dangerous territory, but since hers were focused on the road or perhaps this time she didn't care, they lingered there for quite some time. *Never mind.*

CHAPTER THREE

Zionastra Incorporated, San Francisco, CA
July 16th, 2079, 2127h

"Is there a reason why you parked your car so closely to my company's complex?" Armstrong asked Liszt as they got out of the vehicle. She gave him no immediate reply; instead she merely tossed him a confident smirk over her shoulder and continued to walk towards the front of the building. Seconds later, he pressed the issue as he followed her. "I asked you a valid question." There was no flirtation whatsoever in that statement; in fact, it was pretty grave.

"Who said it was my car?"

"Wha ... wait a minute ... ?!" His voice rose an octave in surprise as he tried to figure this out.

"You probably didn't notice what I was doing with my magnafone because you were occupied, but that's why it took so long for me to get into the car. I was hacking the system. And if you hadn't plonked my magnafone out of the window, I would have detonated the car as soon as we were safely out of the vicinity. I had previously rigged it with charges to blow."

"Did you leave the car unlocked?"

"Of course."

"Then I'm sure that whoever will be having a joyride in it will have a lot more problems than just the cops to worry about," he chuckled. "I guarantee that a ride like that will be gone, even in this neighborhood in probably ten minutes or less."

The doors opened automatically for them, and the guard at the front desk, Manny Rodriguez, gave a friendly waive to Armstrong. "Hey, Nestor. Who's the hot mamacita?" He made a little purr like a cat, and Armstrong gave him a smug look as he stopped by the bureau.

"All right, Manny, hand the fifty over now."

"What?" the Latino feigned innocence. "I thought that it only costed me twenty bucks whenever I was wrong about a woman you brought through that door."

"Make it seventy, then. You owe me for that bet with the big cheese; there weren't any pictures on his desk." *Did he even graduate from high school?*

"As well as an apology for such a misogynistic comment and animalistic behavior," Liszt seethed.

"Wow, she's feisty, Nestor. I like her already, even if she doesn't belong to you," Manny continued his harmless assault and reached into his back pocket for his wallet.

"She doesn't," Liszt returned coldly and snatched the money from him. She then began to head towards the elevator. "Jou ou naai," she mumbled under her breath.

"I don't guess you're gonna be spending that on her anytime soon," Rodriguez continued as soon as she was out of earshot.

"We'll see," Armstrong responded gently and patted his acquaintance on the arm. He then pursued Liszt to the lift. "Sorry about that. What'd you call him, by the way?"

She gave him the fifty dollar bill and pocketed the twenty. "If you truly mean it, then you'll have to earn the rest of it back. Let's just say that I returned his complimentary retort towards me as we walked through the door."

Just when he was about to push the call button near his ear, Armstrong's fingers began to tingle as his phone 'rang'. "This is Armstrong. What's up, Boss?"

"Plans have changed as I warned you earlier, Armstrong," McGregor's sincere voice buzzed throughout his ears. "I assume you've arrived back at the office with our friend."

"Yep."

"Good, now get out of San Francisco and come to my house in Palo Alto."

"Oh. I see. We might have some trouble with transportation."

"How's that? You took your motorcycle to Sondheim's complex, yes?"

"I didn't use it to get back; the details are a bit . . . difficult to explain all at once, sir."

"Fine. Get up to the roof. Charles will meet you there in five," McGregor gruffly responded.

"Shouldn't I return my equipment to the armory?"

"Tomorrow morning. It's my equipment, Mr. Armstrong, and I don't give a damn that it's still in your possession right now. All I want is Liszt and that burner. Now get up to the roof pronto." He ended the call without so much of a goodbye.

"Not much on manners, is he?" Liszt inquired with a slightly arched eyebrow.

"No, he's not. But I can't argue with the man who signs my paychecks."

"For now, you mean."

"A little suspicion is healthy, Liszt; a lot is paranoia. I think you just crossed over that line." They stepped into the elevator, and he scanned his eye to give them the clearance to go to the roof. "And I think you also owe me an explanation for why you made me leave my forty-five thousand dollar motorcycle to sit next to Sondheim Incorporated for the weekend."

"Not . . . not right now. But one day . . . I might." Her words were laced with pain more than anything else, and he wisely chose not to pursue the matter any longer.

An hour later, McGregor's private helicopter landed upon a pad in the woods. The pilot Charles instructed them how to get to the mansion, which was about a quarter of a mile east of their position. "So have you ever been to your boss' private estate before?" Liszt inquired after they had spent the last ten minutes walking silently side by side.

"Nope, first time for me."

"I appreciate what you did for me back there . . . at Sondheim Incorporated. I know that threw a spanner into your plans." Her tone was not business-like at all but rather soft like a plush pillow or rug.

"I'm flexible," he said with a shrug and avoided stepping into a puddle. "But understand that if we ever have to work together again, *I'll* be the one in charge."

"Did I touch a sensitive nerve a few hours ago? Do you have difficulty following orders from a woman?"

He swallowed some saliva down his throat and exhaled slowly. "No, I just think that since your safety is still my objective, that *I* should be the one to give orders, not the opposite way 'round."

"Fair enough. To be honest, though, I do wonder if a part of you liked it."

Armstrong gave her no reply as they made their way up the marble steps of the grand mansion. Before either of them could ring the doorbell, a man in an evening tuxedo opened the door. "Welcome, Mr. Armstrong and Ms. Liszt. My name is Lester. Would you care to freshen up before meeting with Mr. McGregor?"

"Freshen up as in take a shower?" Armstrong inquired. The butler nodded. "Well, neither of us brought a change of clothes."

"Mr. McGregor has many suitable things for the both of you to wear. If you'd be so kind as to not lock your bathroom doors or perhaps leave your soiled things upon your bed, I will collect them in order to ascertain your appropriate sizes. And then of course, they will be laundered, pressed, and ready for you in the morning," Lester informed them.

"I for one am not going to complain. This day has been too damn long," Liszt stated with a nod. "I could use some steam to relieve some stress that's been settling into my back."

"Perhaps you'd also like a massage later this evening. We have a licensed therapist on call."

"That won't be necessary; the shower will be more than adequate." She held up her hands, and he led them to their bedrooms.

"Mr. McGregor has asked that you both join him in the study in approximately half an hour's time for a night cap. From here, just go down the stairs and make a right at the bottom. That'll be the library; head straight through there, and the study is just across from it. Have a pleasant stay."

With that, he made his exit and left them alone again. "So, how difficult is it for you to get out of that . . . uniform?" she innocently asked.

"Oh, you mean Spidey?" Armstrong glanced down at his suit. "I've never had the pleasure of a speed test. Was that an invitation?" He flashed her an impudent smile.

"Perhaps a bit of a challenge. If you can beat me down to the study after taking a rather long shower in less than that half an hour, I'll consider giving you that twenty back that I stole from you earlier."

"You're on." Without another second to lose, he bolted into the bedroom and slammed the door in her face.

As the warm water poured down his back to soothe his aching muscles, Armstrong became plagued by several doubts. What if McGregor simply did just want what Sondheim had? Was he just some kind of pawn in a game of chess? Could Penelope Liszt be right about her suspicions?

Well, I do trust Honda; he's been reliable and fair to me as well as everyone else in our department. Maybe he has the same doubts that I do and just hasn't shared it with anyone yet for fear of losing his job.

He snapped himself out of his inner conflict as he remembered that he was being timed, finished his shower, and hopped out of the bathroom. A white terrycloth robe and a pair of silk slippers were neatly sitting upon his immaculately made bed. A note was attached to the robe stating that an appropriate suit of clothing would be delivered to the bedroom in an hour's time. If the door were closed, then the clothes would be set upon the knob.

Armstrong padded down the stairs, sped through the library, and made it just in time to see McGregor handing Liszt a glass of red wine. "Damn."

She gave him a raised eyebrow in return.

"What's your pleasure, Armstrong?" McGregor demanded.

"Dirty gin martini, no ice, two olives," he replied with a sigh.

"Beefeaters or Tanqueray?"

"Surprise me."

"Well, the Tanqueray's already open," the man responded as bent down to take a glance upon his bottles beneath the bar. "Was there something troubling you?"

"No, I just . . ." Armstrong stole a look across the room at Liszt, who was currently tasting her wine and pretending to be oblivious to their conversation. "I never figured that a woman would take a shorter shower than I is all."

"Humph." McGregor poured some olive juice from a jar into the jigger as well as some vermouth. "Times are changing, aren't they?"

"What're you drinking?" Armstrong directed his question towards her.

"A Merlot from the Sonoma valley. I can't remember the name; would you care to try some?" She sauntered over towards him. The scent of whatever kind of shower gel or bath oil she used completely filled his nose. His heart started to pound a little faster in his chest now due to her proximity and the pleasant odor wafting into his nostrils from her skin.

"I think I'll pass for now, but thanks anyway." What was that scent? Lavender? Jasmine? He wasn't very good with flowers.

"I know that this has been an extraordinary day for the both of you, so in advance, thank you for your cooperation and being willing to meet me here," McGregor announced after he handed Armstrong his drink in a martini glass. He grabbed his snifter of brandy and led them over to a couple of very comfortable cloth sofas.

The two of them sat upon a love seat, while McGregor sat upon a tall straight back chair. The decor of the room was a harsh chestnut; the furniture here was all maroon. Armstrong briefly wondered if anyone had been killed in here.

"Without any further ado, let's have that burner, Ms. Liszt," McGregor announced and stretched out his hand towards her.

"Before I hand this over to you, I think it's only fair that you be more forthcoming with Mr. Armstrong here," she said with an obstinate tone. "You've left out some key details about what's on this cell phone, and he should hear the recording for himself."

"Do you know what a pawn is, Ms. Liszt?"

Son of a bitch, Armstrong's mind cursed.

"Don't lecture me about corporate espionage, Mr. McGregor. I stipulated that I would come to you with evidence on my own accord. Nothing in our agreement says that I absolutely have to relinquish my evidence towards you. In fact, I could just take this over to the San Francisco Police Department . . .—" She put down her glass onto the coffee table in front of them and arose.

"We don't need to involve them, at least not yet," McGregor responded softly and held up his hand. "Please do sit down, Ms. Liszt."

Why is he so anxious not to involve the police? He said something about having some leverage with them.

"Only if you interface this with some audio equipment so that *everyone* in this room can hear this."

"And sir, we also happen to owe her a new magnafone. I had to dispose of her other one so that Sondheim's security team couldn't track us," Armstrong interjected.

"It seems that I am at an impasse here," McGregor insinuated and swirled the brandy around in his glass. He finally took a large gulp from it, stared down his current opponents, and nodded. "We'll proceed as you'd like, Ms. Liszt. The tray that's opening out of the stereo system will accommodate the audio from the expendable cell phone." He gestured to his left with his head, and she placed the miniature electronic device into it. Seconds later, the slot closed and the call began.

"I'm pleased to hear about your results, Quinn Sondheim," a voice that did not quite sound human began the conversation. "Tell me, what has your success rate been?"

"One hundred percent, thanks to your help, Mercury," Sondheim responded. "I've opened two more facilities across the country now, and we are currently building another upon the east coast. I must admit, though, it took us more than fifty tries at first to correctly synthesize that cure."

"A long road, yes?"

"Yeah, and I can't tell you how many people have died during . . . even once you gave me this hope. We used the most severe cases to try and get the best results."

"Think of the lives that you are currently saving. It does you no good to mourn the dead."

"But it's not right to just callously shove them aside."

"Altruism does not win wars."

"This isn't a war, it's a disease that kills!"

"Personally investing yourself in a cause like that weakens you." Mercury hesitated before speaking again, possibly to consider how harsh his half of the conversation had been. "But I suppose that it is admirable to show mercy later on."

"How much later if not now?!"

"Let us not speak of this any more; you are becoming too emotional, and it does not serve the purpose of this contact."

"You're right; I'm sorry." There was a grand pause. "Was the palladium and iridium of good quality for your needs?"

"It was adequate, but we will require more."

"My contacts are doing the best that they can; we cannot mine it any faster than we are right now without attracting attention to Bethesda right now."

Armstrong noticed McGregor scribbling that name down hurriedly on his magnafone.

"You have until the end of this solar month to make the quota," Mercury coldly stated. That was the end of the audio, and the tray opened itself back up.

Liszt removed the burner from the slot, enclosed it back in the petri dish, and handed it over to McGregor. "I ran through every name that I possibly could in our company and found only one person with the last name

Mercury. He was a custodian and seemed completely bewildered when I asked him if he'd ever personally spoken to Mr. Sondheim over a cell phone."

"It's probably a pseudonym," Armstrong guessed and lifted the martini up to his lips to drink. "I didn't recognize that man's accent. What about travel records? Could we get a hold of someone through U.S. Customs? Do we know anything about the other number?"

"I could have Nathan analyze it," McGregor nodded. "And yes, I do know someone from the U.S. embassy . . ."

"That won't be necessary," Liszt said as she shook her head. "I already had that done, the analysis I mean . . . and the lab technician couldn't identify it. Maybe . . . we're not alone out here in the galaxy like so many people have thought."

"What?!" Armstrong cried out.

"Pure conjecture, Ms. Liszt."

"All right, then have your own damned scientist analyze it and come up with a valid contradiction," she snapped back and consumed some of her wine.

"What about this Bethesda? Was Sondheim talking about the naval base in Washington, D.C.? Or the city in Maryland?" Armstrong inquired.

"Hope of Bethesda is the name of the laundering business that Sondheim uses for his EFTs. That could be a lead for the name of the mining company that they're talking about. Unfortunately, I wasn't able to extract that information before I left," Liszt informed them with a shake of her head.

"I'm sending a message to Honda to do so right now . . . or well, since it is rather late, that can wait until tomorrow, of course." McGregor's eyes went to the old fashioned analog grandfather clock that sat in a corner. He finished his dictation into his magnafone while his interlocutors quietly sipped their drinks. "Send message now."

"So what's next for us, Boss?" Armstrong asked.

"When Honda finds something worthwhile, I'll send you to him. Then he'll decide what to do; I'm leaving the choice up to him. But I'd imagine that you'll probably be involved in a recon mission with this Bethesda corporation."

"I'd like to offer my continued assistance," Liszt piped in.

"That won't be necessary," McGregor brushed her off with the shake of his head. "You've done more than enough on your behalf, Ms. Liszt, and I assure you, you will be compensated for it monetarily as of Monday morning."

"That's not the reason why I'm doing this." Her eyes narrowed. "It's *never* been about money for me; I could have brought this to Sondheim myself and blackmailed him if it were. Neither do I fear Wooster at all; I could have removed him from his position without any trouble whatsoever."

"Then why didn't you?" Armstrong shrugged.

"There was a lack of time for me to fully develop a plan. But regardless of that, how intelligent is it of your employer to refuse a second offer of alliance?"

"Don't insult me. You may not fear your former superior, but I will *not* tolerate insubordination," McGregor returned calmly and plonked his glass down on the table beside him. "Or threats."

"Or what? You'll have your little 'pawn' strangle me?" Liszt pointed to Nestor, who bit his lip. McGregor's eyes flooded themselves with fury, and he pursed his lips together very firmly.

He closed his eyes and silently counted to five. "You make a valid point, Ms. Liszt. Very well; I will give you an answer in the morning."

"Good. You'll find that I'm a woman of a great many talents." She finished her wine and bid them both a good night before leaving the study.

"Sir, can I ask a favor from you?" Armstrong questioned his boss.

"Please do make it fast. That woman is giving me an unbearable headache," McGregor growled.

"That's completely understandable, sir. I'd like to do this reconnaissance mission alone, please." McGregor's eyes made contact with his as if to ask him 'why'; Armstrong continued his plea. "It's not that I don't find her company unsatisfactory, but . . ."

"Your request has been heard, Armstrong. I also realize why you prefer to be the lone wolf that you've always been here at Zionastra. But you may have to put that unpleasant situation that happened to you in the past."

"That's why it's a request, sir. I'll do whatever you order me to, but . . ."

"This decision is not yet final, Armstrong. I'll sleep on it, and I suggest that you do the same now." McGregor took his brandy out of the study with him, and they parted ways.

When Armstrong arrived back in his bedroom, he was rather surprised to find Liszt leaning against the frame of his door. He tried not to let that show on his face. "Want another chance to earn that twenty back?" she questioned him.

"It's becoming less and less likely that *that'll* ever happen, with the way you make bets," he snorted.

"This one is a no-brainer."

"I'm listening."

"Want to bet if there are bugs in our rooms already?"

"If I say yes, does that mean that I get the Andrew J. back?" He crossed his arms against his chest and joined her on the opposite side.

"Just remember what I said about your employer."

"Duly noted." A part of him was tempted to ask if she wanted to give McGregor's listeners a show, but as another thought struck him, he brushed it away. Before he could say another word, she had disappeared into her own room.

He pulled out his magnafone, searched for a video file, turned the device's speakers as loud as possible, and began to sweep the room for any bugs. Finding one near the night stand, he let the magnafone sit upon his bed while he went into his bathroom to make a phone call. The sounds of a moaning woman in ecstasy and a man grunting with pleasure *in flagrante delecto* began to fill up his bedroom.

"Hey, Young, it's Armstrong. What? Oh, no, for once, that's not me. Very droll, you overweight dwarf, I'm using it to mask my call to you. No, I can't say where I am right now other than the fact that those voices you hear in the background are simulated and not actually happening where I am. Listen, I've got a favor to ask of you."

Armstrong paused as he listened to the other half of the conversation. "I can't talk about that. Now, can you do me a huge favor and impound my motorcycle for me? It's sitting three blocks to the west of Sondheim Incorporated in an alley. I'll come pick it up either tomorrow or on Sunday. How much? You drive a hard bargain, man. Yeah, I know, I owe you. Thanks."

Just as he was about to turn off the magnafone's sound, a knock came to his door. *Maybe I'd better leave that going if it's Liszt.* "Coming," he announced and opened it.

The visitor was definitely not Liszt, although she was female. She had long, straight blonde hair and a very enticing pair of slate blue eyes. A smile had previously come across her face, but after he had opened the door, a look of puzzlement now crossed it. "Oops," he chuckled, ran over to the bed, and muted the audio coming from the magnafone. "Sorry about that."

She couldn't have been much more than twenty-five or twenty-six, but again, who knew with all that gene therapy these days?

"Hi, Mr. Armstrong, I'm Irene, Mr. McGregor's niece. I just came to see if you had everything that you'd be needing for the evening." The beam came back again.

He honestly felt a little unnerved and a bit feverish; if he were a bar of chocolate, he would have truly melted away into a puddle at her feet. "Irene, huh? That's sweet of you, but I think I'll be okay."

"Are you sure? Perhaps a pair of earphones would be in order?" She nearly giggled, which caused him to blush bashfully.

"Your uncle's listening devices needed some entertainment," he joked.

When her eyebrows knit together with concern, he shook his head. "Never mind that now. Seriously, I'll be fine for tonight I think. Hopefully, I'll eventually get some clothes to wear in the morning."

"Don't worry; I'm sure Lester's put the rest of the staff to work on your attire. You know," she folded her arms around herself, "it's odd that you're here. I mean, I've lived in this mansion for about sixteen years now, but Uncle's *never* invited any of his employees over for anything more than dinner. He must trust you a lot."

Armstrong leaned forward and began to whisper into her ear. "So how well do you know him, then?" She tilted her head to the side, not quite understanding what he wanted to know in response. "Would he be more interested in revealing the truth to someone rather than making money?"

"There are *many* things that I don't know about him, unfortunately," Irene replied at the same volume and lowered her eyes. She pondered his question a bit longer, pursed her lips together, and finally went on. Their entire conversation was now but a whisper. "He's been a little cruel to me with his words but has *never* raised a hand to me or treated me unfairly."

"How cruel?"

"Well, I did ask his opinion once about a dress that I wore to the prom, and he is a brutally honest man. I learned never to ask that question again."

"No doubt."

The corners of her mouth began to pull away to make another smile, but then they retreated as she remembered something else. Her face became morbidly serious.

"There's a part of the house where *no* one but my uncle can go." She touched her fingers to her lips idly as she thought. "I've often wondered what secrets he keeps there but don't dare to ask him because he's been so kind to take me in."

"He took you in?"

"My dad . . . he . . . used to hurt me. And my mom used to drink . . . a lot, so much that she didn't even feel it when he beat the both of us."

Armstrong's fists curled up at his sides. "I hope the bastard was sent away for life, but knowing how our goddamned justice system works, he probably will only get about six years if that." One of his balled up fists slammed into the wall. "That's one of the reasons why I left the system; too many sick minded freaks were released all too soon on account of their quote good behavior."

She lifted her shoulders up in surrender. "I don't know. My uncle dealt with that. I haven't heard about either of them ever since he came to take me away from them."

"Well, it's good to know that I'm not working for a completely heartless man."

"And I know that he owns the company you work for of course, but I have no real idea of what you do, you know, with all that medical technology. Just be careful, Mr. Armstrong." She gave him one last winning smile that practically mollified his heart. Irene steered the conversation back to a normal decibel level. "It was nice to meet you, and I hope that you like it here."

"Meeting you has certainly been a good part of it." He gave her a long wink.

"Maybe I'll see you at breakfast, then?"

"Count on it. I'm an early riser, though."

"How early? Want to go for a run around the track?"

"Yeah, that sounds great," Armstrong nodded. "6:45 okay with you?"

"Sure. I'll meet you here. Finding it's a bit tricky. Good night."

"Don't let the bed bugs bite."

"I'm sorry?" She scratched her forehead with confusion.

"I'll tell you in the morning what that means."

"Oh, I won't be able to sleep now—I'll just look it up on wiki." Irene spun around on her heel and left.

The strangest things happen to me, I swear. Five hours ago, I met a cold but pushy woman who ordered me all over the battlefield. And just now I ran into a woman who could probably outshine the sun with her smile.

CHAPTER FOUR

Mcgregor Mansion, Palo Alto, CA
July 17th, 2079, 0645h

The knock came to his door, and it was Irene. She was once again grinning from ear to ear and handed him a pair of cargo shorts as well as a t-shirt. "Hi. Lester originally was going to give you a suit with a tie, but I told him that we were going running this morning."

"Good morning to you, too," he yawned. "Are you a morning person?"

"Well, to tell you the truth, I woke up half an hour ago and had some mate already." She gathered some of her blonde locks up into her hands and formed it into a loose but sloppy ponytail. "Believe you me, I even look worse when I get up."

"Thanks for the clothes." He didn't even bother to close the door for privacy, took off his robe, slid into the shorts, and threw the t-shirt over his head. "Have you any—"

Her other hand appeared from behind her back with a pair of sneakers and white socks. "Running shoes?" she laughed.

"Uh, yeah, those." Armstrong took them from her and fitted his feet with them. "I'm not gonna ask how he knew what size of shoes I wear."

She made a gesture to the freshly shined combat boots in the hallway. "These belong to you, don't they?"

"Oh, that's what happened to them. That guy gets around." He rested a palm against his forehead. "Well, shall we, Irene?"

"Sounds good." Armstrong had originally planned to bring his magnafone to entertain him as he ran, but maybe she wanted to talk.

Once they got to the track, both of them did a tiny bit of stretching. Then, suddenly, she was off like the wind. "Come on, sleepy head," she teased him.

"You don't miss a beat, do you?" he wondered and took off.

"We'll start off slow if you'd like to warm up."

"You're not a personal trainer, are you?"

"Me? Oh hell, no." She waved a hand dismissively at the comment. "I'm a dancer."

"What kind of dancing?"

"Well, I did start off later than most kids, but I do a little of everything."

"You don't have a favorite?"

"Sure. I love to do classic ballroom dancing, but outside of that one TV show, you just don't see too much of that anymore. Oh, and I can clog dance like nobody's business."

"Clog dancing, eh?"

She began to pick up the pace. "Yep."

"How about a tango?" he huffed as he caught up with her eventually. "And what's the rush?"

"I can tango; it's very sensual. But if your partner doesn't make a visual connection to you . . ." She shook her head and let the sentence trail off. "Come *on*. Men like to chase women, don't they?"

"Oh, is that why you're speeding up?" Armstrong chuckled. "I'm game."

"You sure you can keep up, Mr. Armstrong?"

He was panting now. "Damn . . . it's Nestor, by the way."

"Like from the Iliad and the Odyssey? I love Greek mythology." She now had trouble breathing normally now, too. "But I prefer the Iliad."

For the next fifteen minutes, they ran hard around the track, and although she had been leading, she let him gauge the cool down. "Tell me something, Irene," he breathed.

"What's that?"

"I went to a rehearsal once and was able to watch a bunch of you all work the wood. Why the hell do you all shout out 5, 6, 7, 8 to start a step? Doesn't music go 1, 2, 3, 4?"

"Ha! I forgot we do that!" she guffawed. "Probably to avoid confusion with the musicians, I guess, if they're also in the same rehearsal. But not all music goes 1, 2, 3, 4, you know. There are waltzes, two steps, rhumbas, mambos, and—"

"I think I'm gonna get lost before you elaborate too much further, so let's just stop there, Irene. But thanks for telling me that."

"Sure, no prob. Where were you, by the way? Maybe I've got some friends in the company you saw."

"I can't talk about it, sorry. Used to be a cop for SFPD."

"Hmm, that figures." They slowed down quite a bit more.

"How's that?"

"Well, you mentioned something about being disgusted with how the justice system works, so I figured you were in some kind of law enforcement, but I had no actual clue until you just told me."

By the time they finished, there were two towels waiting for them on a bench as well as two glasses filled to the brim with ice cold water. "Damn, I could almost get used to this," Armstrong shook his head as he wiped the sweat off of himself.

"I never have," she chortled. "That's why I brought your clothes up to you. Lester wanted to do it himself, but I told him to go make breakfast for my uncle." She rolled her eyes. "In fact, I never let him make mine. He dotes on me far too much."

"Maybe he thinks of you as his daughter or something." He brought the glass up to his lips and quenched his thirst. "And what's mate, by the way? You mentioned drinking some of that earlier."

"I don't care for the way he makes toast, either. Lester doesn't let it sit in the machine long enough for my tastes; I want toast, not warm bread," Irene informed him as she also toweled herself off. "Mate is a type of hot tea that's popular in certain parts of South America, like Argentina, Uruguay, and Paraguay. A fellow friend of mine introduced me to it; actually, the first tango partner I had was from Argentina, as a matter of fact. I swear, his frame was fierce! I've been addicted to mate ever since."

He rolled his neck around his shoulders and stripped himself of his t-shirt. "Ah, that's much better."

She caught a glimpse of his finely toned muscles through the glass as she drank her water down quickly. "I have to agree." Irene let out another heavy exhale. "But it's *so* unfair that guys can do that anytime they want."

"Who's stopping you from doing the same; we're alone out here, aren't we?" He gave her a smirk, and she slapped him playfully with her towel.

"Can you find your way back? I'm gonna go take a shower and do some stretches."

"I'll manage . . . somehow." His face turned into a semi-legitimate pout. "You know, men are supposedly helpless when it comes to directions."

"That's actually quite the opposite of what I've heard," she commented wryly with the raise of an eyebrow. "I'll catch you later, Nestor." Before he could complain, she energetically spun around upon her heel and took off.

Half an hour later, he returned to the mansion's backyard carrying his towel, glass, and shirt to find an impeccably dressed Penelope Liszt sitting under the shelter of an umbrella eating her breakfast. "Morning," he greeted her.

"Yes, it is," she mused and glanced upward at him briefly. "Our host has gone and left us already. He left a note with his servant saying that I could accompany you and do whatever I feel is necessary. And on a more positive note, your boss will reluctantly reimburse me for whatever expenses this mission further incurs."

Why do I have a feeling that some of that might be a bit exaggerated?

"So uh . . . what do you say to sharing that cup of coffee between the two of us?" he nearly stammered.

She noticed that her glass of orange juice was nearly empty. "Sounds lovely. There's enough breakfast here for two, actually . . . if you like eggs benedict and authentic English bacon."

"I'll go in and grab the coffee as well as the mugs, then." Liszt turned her head and squinted behind herself as she watched Lester make an about face and head into the kitchen.

"I think he may be bringing it out for us already," she said.

About one minute later, Lester brought out a tray with a bone white carafe as well as two china cups bearing a similar hue towards them. "Guess I'll just . . . have a seat, then," Armstrong muttered helplessly and did so.

"Good morning to you, Mr. Armstrong, and again to you, Ms. Liszt," Lester declared as he began to pour the coffee. "I trust your morning run with Miss McGregor was invigorating?"

Liszt had been chewing her food non-stop, but that last question gave her a moment of pause. Three seconds later, though, she went back enjoying the warm food in her mouth. "Thank you, Lester, that'll be all. And we'll take the trays in when we're done. You don't need fuss over us like this," she informed him.

"It would be my pleasure to serve you, Ms. Liszt. This is Mr. McGregor's summer home; he spends most of the week in the city in his townhouse, so it's nice to have someone around to wait upon," he responded with a slight bow.

"Still, I don't think either of us are used to . . . well . . . being served," Armstrong returned quietly as he watched Lester pour the coffee.

"Cream or sugar, sir?"

"Please, Lester, really . . . we'll be okay." He held up a hand to stop him, and the butler merely handed him the cup. Lester then did the same for Liszt and then took off as quick as a wink. "I was right, wasn't I? Or did you grow up with a few more privileges than I?"

"Actually, we did have servants in the house where I grew up. However, I left home when I was sixteen and haven't bothered with them ever since," she responded coolly and blew some steam off of her cup. "So . . . about that nickname you gave me . . ."

"Oh, that," he laughed through his nose and stirred some cream into his cup. "Haven't you ever seen those old Clint Eastwood films?"

"Who's Clint Eastwood?" She drank her coffee straight up without any sugar or cream.

"I'll take that as a no, then." He paused to stir the hot liquid before attempting to drink it. "He was an actor and a director from the last century that pretty much made a fictitious cop from San Francisco infamous by the name of Dirty Harry."

"I see. Was he corrupt?"

"No, he just didn't care to do things by the book. He got the job done and would do almost anything that it took to get the bad guy. There are a lot of famous lines from his movies . . . the first one in particular. You might recognize one if you heard it. Oh, and he also carried around this huge .44 Smith and Wesson old fashioned revolver."

"A revolver? My, this movie does sound old." She used both her fork and knife to slice up her bacon. "But mildly intriguing, I suppose. And what, out of curiosity made my actions similar enough to this rogue police officer to give me the nickname of 'Dirty Harriet'?"

"That first long walk you made down the hallway. Although, you didn't shout out 'halt' at first to the bad guys or have a hot dog in your mouth at the time, you still calmly strolled down it like you were having a normal day and nailed all the tangos without missing a beat." He shoved a forkful of eggs into his mouth.

"Why would I have a hot dog in my mouth?"

Armstrong finished his bite and washed it down with some coffee. "Oh, well, Dirty Harry was having lunch at the time of the robbery. The crooks were trying to knock off a bank down the street, and he told the cook to call the cops. Then he took the hot dog down the street in hand, pulled out his gun, and yelled 'halt'. Naturally, none of them did and began to open fire at him. So he strutted down the street just like you and took 'em out while finishing his last bite of the hot dog. Sorry, wait a minute, I'm wrong."

"Oh? Which part did you leave out?"

"I didn't leave anything out; I made a mistake. Whereas *you* chose to take the crooks out, Dirty Harry just wounded them."

"Does that make me a bad person? I was just removing a threat to you and myself. They were also under orders from Wooster to kill us."

"Don't put words into my mouth." He shot her a glare and continued to eat.

"So, Lester mentioned a 'Miss' McGregor." When Armstrong didn't give her any kind of reaction other than a cursory glance, she went on. "Who is she to him . . . a daughter . . . a ward . . . a niece, perhaps?"

"She's his niece, though she didn't say which side of the family he belonged to."

"Is she pleasant?"

"I'll let you talk to her and find out for yourself."

"You don't have to be so snippy, you know." She took another drink from her coffee and let her fingers tap rhythmically against the cup.

"You don't seem to be the type to want to make small talk."

"Sorry, I thought that that was why you wanted to have the coffee with me this morning." Liszt's eyes lost whatever warmth had been present. "I'm perfectly satisfied to eat in silence."

He rubbed his fingers over his forehead to try and hide his embarrassment. "Forgive me, Liszt, it's just been a long while since I . . . well since I . . . spoke with someone so casually that I work with."

"You were making a lot of jokes yesterday; I find that difficult to swallow."

"Like I said, I just say that stuff to relieve some stress. And I think we were under a quite a bit yesterday, weren't we?"

"Yes, we were." She stopped tapping her fingers against the cup and drained the remainder of the liquid that was there in it.

"So tell me about yourself, Liszt."

"If you'd like, you can call me Penelope." Her eyes made contact with his.

"Liszt is a bit shorter, although Penelope is a pretty elegant name."

"Thank you." Liszt combined some of the eggs as well as a cut of bacon into her mouth.

"I'm guessing Penny isn't one of my choices?"

She rolled her eyes and swallowed her food. "I'd rather go back to hearing Dirty Harriet first."

"Yeah, but you don't carry a .44 Magnum revolver." He continued to eat his breakfast.

"I suppose since we'll be working together now, that we should disclose some information to one another to gain some trust," she observed. "Since I already know some things about you, it's only fair. Well, you know that I was raised in Cape Town, South Africa and left home when I was sixteen. That was by choice; I had a . . . disagreement with my step mother." When he wisely chose not to pry, she went on. "I've worked for Sondheim Incorporated for the last seven years now. Before that, I received a degree from university in criminology and minored in political science."

"How did you afford college?"

"I had some money saved up before I left home, and I worked my way through university."

"Doing what?" When she hesitated to give him an answer, he waved his hand in front of himself. "Never mind, it's none of my business."

"It isn't? It was nothing illegal, I assure you." She paused to take one last bite of her plate of food. "I worked at a gun smithing shop and a firing range."

He gave her a rogue grin. "Then maybe Dirty Harriet *should* stay."

"And what about you? Would you prefer that I call you Armstrong or Nestor?"

"Whichever one rolls off your tongue faster for you; it doesn't matter to me."

"Nestor . . . hmm . . ." She ran a finger slowly around her mouth a few times as she thought and crossed one leg over the other. The outfit that Lester had given her was another business suit; this one did not have pants but rather a skirt. This one was a light cream, which did accentuate her soft tanned skin rather nicely, he thought. He also didn't mind the fact that he could see more of her shapely legs now.

"Now I remember where I know that name. He was the son of Neleus, king of Pylos and also one of Jason's infamous Argonauts, yes?" Liszt recalled.

"He also led an assault on Troy."

"Were either of your parents Greek?"

"I . . . I don't know." He cleared his throat and drank some more of his coffee. "I never knew them; I was raised on a Native American reservation as a kid. One of the chiefs taught me how to be a marksman, and I never went to college. I joined their local force when I was eighteen, then came to San Francisco three years later."

"Dances With Wolves, then? I've seen that film, although I didn't care much for it myself."

He shook his head. "I'm not big on Kevin Costner, so, no. That name's not gonna stick well."

"Well, I'll find one for you soon enough." Her eyes searched his with intrigue. "And why exactly is your outfit called 'Spidey'? Is that from Spiderman?"

"Yeah, I grew up reading those comic books non-stop. I could never get enough of Peter Parker's adventures," he remarked with a smile.

"Tiger."

"I'm sorry?"

"I read some of those as well, too, and I saw those films. Mary Jane called Peter 'tiger' for short, didn't she? How does that suit you?"

A short rumble went through his throat as he thought, almost like a purr.

Liszt gave him a closed mouth beam and switched legs. "I think that'll do rather nicely for you."

"So, did this letter from McGregor have any more orders?"

"Yes, he'd like for us to go visit your office to meet Honda and debrief him about the mission personally. He will likely also be able to give us some intel about this Bethesda company."

"Was there a deadline given to us?"

Her business tone returned as did her professional mask. "His very words were 'sometime today', so I'll take that as meaning that we have twenty-four hours or less to get our act together," Liszt explained. "I'd imagine that you'll probably like to get cleaned up and make contact with your immediate supervisor. Then when you're finished . . ." she cut herself off. "Sorry. I um . . . forgot that I'm not the one in charge here. What I meant to ask was . . . what are your plans?"

"Pretty much what you just said," he chuckled. "But two great minds do think alike. As soon as I've done so, I'll let you know from there. Sound good to you, Harriet?"

She gave him a nod in agreement. "I'll see if I can get in touch with someone about Bethesda myself. There is a scientist in the lab over at Sondheim that I trust very much. She was the one who did that voice analysis I mentioned last night. I'll likely be out on the front porch making those calls. Come find me when you're ready to leave, Tiger."

Liszt arose from her seat, collected her dishes as well as the serving tray for the coffee, and took off back into the house.

Ft. De Soto Beach, St. Petersburg, FL July 17th, 2079, 1002h

The morning humidity was already baking most of the Florida residents and a minute amount of tourists that chose to spend their morning on the beach. However, it did not seem to bother Mercury, who sat underneath a giant white umbrella at a table. A sweating glass of ice sat upon a coaster, and he withdrew a metallic canister from his suit coat pocket. The vendor who had graciously given him both wondered if he wanted a coke with that, but Mercury swept his magnafone across the credit kiosk without another word to pay the full price of the drink.

After he opened the can, Quinn Sondheim approached him. "Mr. Mercury, thank you for being wiling to speak with me." Sondheim removed the sunglasses from his eyes and placed them onto the table. "May I join you?"

Mercury let the can's contents fill the glass and nodded. "Obviously, yes."

Sondheim slid the metallic beach chair back and sat down to face his colleague. "I don't exactly know how to approach this delicate matter since I . . . well . . . ever since we began our unique relationship about two years ago. I also don't want you to think that I'm not grateful for what you've done for me, well, for cancer patients everywhere."

"Are you desiring to put an end to our agreement?"

"No," Sondheim announced without hesitation. "I've just been getting very strange reports of things happening now to the people who have been consuming this elixir."

"What kind of things?" Mercury's face seemed to be devoid of any kind of emotion whatsoever, and he now lifted the glass from the coaster to drink from it.

"Some of my employees used to have the disease, and now many of them have offered to work for me for nothing. Whenever I walk into a room with these former cancer patients, all of them stop whatever they are doing and look at me with this . . . odd kind of reverence. It's very eerie; it's as if they want to start bowing their heads towards me or get down on their knees. Thankfully, none of them have done that."

"They are truly grateful for the service you have rendered to them. That is nothing to be ashamed of, Quinn Sondheim."

The affluent but middle aged human's eyes darted around as if someone had heard Mercury use his full name, but no one seemed to even be paying attention to either of them.

"I'd normally agree with you, Mercury, but the president of Gei Hinnom, the mining company that we use to find those precious materials you need, has begun to suggest that we do this all for practically nothing. Two years ago when I contacted him through Bethesda, he laughed in my face and gave me a very high price. But when I told him that I could help his little six year old boy that had leukemia, his tune changed very quickly. These rare earths, Mercury, are commodities."

The alien finished his drink and grasped the glass in both hands to combat the heat. "How are the settlement plans faring for Mars? Did you share the technology I gave you with your government?"

"Actually, I sent the technology through Bethesda. It's funneling through them to several private corporations who service the government. As a matter of fact, one of the companies is one that I used to work for, Lochsummit

Miller, is heading up the construction for the biometric dome," Sondheim explained.

"I have been truly embroiled whilst overseeing all of the Ochrana's manufacturing facilities; I have not had the time to visit that planet to look."

"As I understand, the progress is slow but steady, and Mars will probably be ready for colonization at the end of this year." Sondheim folded his hands together. "Doing this will enable us to finally be able to breathe a bit more on our overly populated planet. Thirty billion people live here, and thanks to this cure, we've got more people actually living longer lives. Maybe that's why people like McGregor are so against me; they think we're already overrun."

"You have done a very noble thing for your kind, Quinn Sondheim. You deserve to be honored; do not hold back when they sing songs of you or build statues in your honor after you have passed on."

"It doesn't feel like it, though. I'm still making loads of money off of this. There are five treatments each patient must undergo at precise times, and if they miss even one application . . ." He glanced downward at his fingers despondently. "Then all will be for nothing. Have there been any major battles in between the Ochrana and the Feindliche?"

Mercury lifted the glass to press it to his forehead. "Yes. There was an extremely bloody fight not too long ago where I had to make a very difficult decision; I had to choose to leave behind some ground troops upon a planet along with a very high general or save an entire fleet of ships."

"Which did you choose?"

"The fleet, of course. One planet does not matter in an epic war; the Ochrana have colonized at least forty different worlds."

"I wish we could help you."

"You are; you have no idea how much or how far your materials are going. Not only are you assisting us with a great war but also, you are providing jobs to our people and putting food into their families' mouths." He paused to ponder the matter a bit longer and then put the glass onto the table. "It is also best that no one else knows about this deal so that we can win this war. You have kept our business relationship a secret, have you not? No one else knows about us?"

"But isn't it important to ask for allies?"

"Your kind is too primitive to interfere, nor do you understand why the Feindliche need to be eradicated from the galaxy."

"You should talk to some of our military officials; they know threats when they see them and would gladly help the Ochrana out. If we know the Feindliche's weaknesses, we could strike back at them and lend you a hand. No one is invulnerable."

"Must I reiterate what I told you two years ago?! I do not desire to draw the Feindliche's attention towards Earth at all! You are the only point of contact I so desire to use, Quinn Sondheim; do not make me regret my choice." With that final statement, Mercury arose and disappeared from sight.

CHAPTER FIVE

Zionastra Armory and Laboratory
July 17th, 2079, 1249h

"So is this armory completely hidden from the public?" Liszt demanded as she and Armstrong both stepped off of the elevator.

"That's kind of an odd thing to advertise when you're trying to entice people to buy your stock, don't you think?" Armstrong shot back. "Buy our drugs or our tech because we promise to protect your shares with bullets, explosions, or sound waves?"

"Guarantee them, you mean. Talk to your sales department; I'm sure that that's exactly what they say."

"Not interested in those leeches." He rolled his eyes and quickened his step.

Once they strolled into the lab, they immediately heard the sound of a powerful revolver going off; the head of Zionastra security, Vincent Honda was firing a gun with a Smith and Wesson Model 29 at a wooden target. Nathan Falk stood right next to him and beamed proudly as he witnessed the head totally separate from the rest of its body. The next shot caused the two by four plywood to fall backward another ten feet onto the ground.

"Oh, for Pete's sake," Armstrong mumbled and pressed his fingers into his forehead. "I can't believe he did this."

"Why?"

He turned and gave her a sour look. "*That's* modeled exactly like the gun I told you about that Dirty Harry used. And I only mentioned your nickname once in the whole exchange I had with Falk . . ."

As if on cue, Falk signaled them to come closer with his hand with a smile. "How do you like our new weapon, Mr. Honda?" he wondered.

The Asian man lowered the gun and set it down onto a ledge. He rotated both of his wrists and gave Falk one single nod. "Approved. Issue it immediately; was it not for Ms. Liszt's use? Would you care to try out the revolver?"

"I'm flattered." She touched a hand to her chest and agreed. "I prime it by pulling the hammer back first, oweh?"

Honda nodded as he watched her pick up the weapon and feel the balance of the gun in between her hands. She then ran her fingers across the grip, wrapped both hands around it, pulled the hammer back, and took aim at another wooden target that was next to the destroyed one. Two seconds later, it suffered the same fate with another two charges. "Oweh, I like this *very* much."

Liszt gave the gun back to Honda and practically sauntered back over to Falk. "Did you say that you specifically built it for *me*?"

"Well, I modified it, really. Honda already had a copy of it on display near his safe; he handed it to me about three hours ago. There wasn't much to it, really," Falk said with a casual shrug.

"I don't believe this," Armstrong groaned.

"And why not? That 'Spidey' suit was crafted just for you," the Irishman stated and put his hands upon his hips. "I'm guessing that that's going to need to be mended." He pointed to the suit that Armstrong had just pulled out of his backpack. It had more than a few bullet holes in it.

"You don't happen to have a spare, do you? We're expecting to run into some trouble at Bethesda or wherever else we have to go today," Armstrong put on his best charming voice.

Falk disgustedly seized the suit from him and disappeared behind a very large metallic door. "Talk amongst yourselves; I'll be back in a few moments."

Armstrong approached his boss and stuck out his hand. "How're you, sir?"

"I'm doing well, and it looks as if you both came out of there without too much collateral damage," Honda nodded somberly. "The police naturally called me last night to inquire if we had something to do with any of this . . . since there were dead bodies. I warned you about those, Armstrong." His eyes narrowed. "Don't make me regret promoting you."

Armstrong was momentarily tempted to glance in Liszt's direction, but he just placed his hands behind his back and stared straight forward. After what seemed like fifteen years, the grim silence was broken.

"Actually, I'm the one who's responsible," Liszt spoke up and cleared her throat. "Those employees are dead because of me; they were ordered by Wooster to use lethal force. Armstrong didn't kill one person."

"Do you have proof of this, Ms. Liszt?"

She sighed. "I had made recordings of our radio transmissions on my magnafone."

Armstrong winced and bit his lip. "I might have . . . accidentally . . . um . . . dropped it off when we were escaping the Sondheim complex . . . uh . . . somewhere."

"That was to prohibit Wooster's teams from discovering your location, I understand," Honda realized. "That's unfortunate; it would have made things with San Francisco PD a run a bit more smoothly."

"Should I try to go talk to the local precinct's captain to explain it all?"

"McGregor and I will deal with the blowback, Armstrong. Just keep Ms. Liszt here safe in the meanwhile, and we'll discuss your next assignment after Falk gets back with your protective suit."

Falk returned shortly after that and shoved it into Armstrong's chest. "I'd like to teach you a new piece of vocabulary, Nestor, if I may."

"What's that?"

"Duck," was all he said and grunted as he shuffled over towards the new gun.

"Have you given that beauty a name yet?" Liszt inquired.

"No, why don't you christen it, Ms. Liszt?"

"Hmm . . . I think Leontine will do."

Falk picked up the gun and handed it to her. "Fierce as a lion; and you look like you're as strong as a mighty gale, Ms. Liszt. I'm truly inspired."

"Why didn't *I* get to name my gun?" Armstrong's lips formed a mock pout. "And just what does 'luke' mean? It's not Latin for 'light', is it?"

"No, it's from the Norwegian word 'lukke', which means to stop or halt. When you bring back a piece of equipment here that doesn't get damaged or blown to bits, then you can name one of your own damned weapons."

"So, do I need to reload the charges, or will it automatically recharge?" Liszt inquired.

"Aye, it'll recharge; it takes about three to four seconds to do so, so I'd recommend taking some cover first. Or since he seems to enjoy playing the bloody hero, you can just hide behind Mr. Armstrong here." Falk jerked his thumb towards him.

"Now hang on just a minute here . . ." Armstrong began to protest but then stopped when Honda made eye contact with him. "Yes, sir?"

"Let's have a talk in the lounge, you two. It's about one o'clock; no one should be in there from lunch hour now." Honda led the two of them out of the armory and up a staircase. They climbed two floors and arrived in a room that was about fifteen by fifteen feet. A large flatscreen TV monitor hung on the wall, and two love seats sat about eight or nine feet in front of it. Two coffee machines sat on a kitchen counter not too far away from it; one was a simple 'coffee on demand' system, and the other was an expresso as well as a cappuccino maker. One of them hummed noisily while it cleaned itself, and the other was as silent as a grave.

A stack of coffee mugs sat next to the machines as well as some non-dairy creamer, a cup full of plastic red and white stir sticks, and a bowl of sugar packets. Honda meandered over towards the counter, poured himself a cup from the 'coffee on demand' system, and then proceeded to add two packets of sugar into his beverage. "Please, feel free to take some if you'd like, Ms. Liszt. Armstrong can't get enough coffee; I never have to offer."

"I think I had plenty this morning, thank you," she replied noncommittally and sat down upon one of the love seats.

Armstrong filled up his own mug, added some non-dairy creamer, and stirred it in silence. Honda sat on the couch opposite to Liszt, while Armstrong sat down next to her and gently began to stir his extremely hot coffee. "I'm afraid that I do not have much to show for the research I did this morning. However, what I did find is that the laundering company of Sondheim that Ms.

Liszt here has told us about, Hope of Bethesda, has been dropping clients right and left in the past six months."

"What about the mining company?"

"I wasn't able to discover that; you'll have to do that yourselves; their profit margin has stayed the same, though. They may be doing it to accommodate Sondheim Incorporated better."

"Is this front company local?" Armstrong asked.

"It's in Sacramento; that I *do* know," Liszt remarked. "I can get us there if we go to my apartment first."

"We have a little bit of a transportation problem, though, if you might remember," Armstrong reminded her and cleared his throat.

"I'll take you both there; my car is here today," Honda announced. "But first, let's talk a little more." He lifted his mug up to his mouth to drink the steamy beverage before continuing. "The president of Hope of Bethesda, Michael Franklin had his own bout with the disease last year. He was diagnosed with stage two prostate cancer, and now, he only makes trips to his doctor once every six months for a check up."

"That doesn't sound suspicious at *all*," Liszt jeered. "Sounds like a gam."

"It sounds like a correlation, indeed. Try and see if you can convince him to come back here to be medically examined by Falk."

"What kind of means should we use to persuade him?"

"I was just thinking about saying the word 'please' first," Armstrong joked. "I'll just keep that tranquilizer gun with me; does that sound fair, sir?"

"Yes, and please try to keep this extraction subtle," Honda informed them. "It wouldn't do for the populace to witness an unconscious executive being hauled out of his own building over your shoulder, Armstrong."

"How about we blow something up for a distraction?" the ex-cop offered.

"And keep the property damage to a minimum, too, please," Honda said with a sigh. "You caused two major accidents in your escapade with Ms. Liszt here."

"Two? I only saw one."

"It happened just afterward, Armstrong. I saw it in the rearview mirror but chose not to say anything about it because I didn't want to distract you," Liszt reported. "Besides, it wasn't nearly as impressive as the first one. Well, shall we be off now?"

"In about five minutes, yes," Honda agreed and made a gesture to his mug. "I'd like to finish my coffee here."

"As would I," Armstrong said with a nod.

"Then I'll venture back to the armory to go reacquaint myself with Leontine. Come get me when you're ready, Tiger," she commented and arose. Upon her exit, she threw Armstrong a smirk over her shoulder.

"Tiger?" Honda's eyes went towards his underling.

"I called her Dirty Harriet once," Armstrong replied. "So I guess she decided to come up with a nickname for me of sorts, too."

"Are you two getting along now?"

"To a point, sure. We had our moments yesterday, and we probably will again today, but I'm dealing with it, sir." He paused to consume more of his coffee. "Mr. Honda, may I ask you a question?"

"Regarding what, Armstrong?"

"Do you think that McGregor wants this cure for himself, or do you think that he just wants to bring Sondheim down?"

Honda pondered the matter in his mind for a little while and scratched his cheek thoughtfully. "Honestly, Armstrong . . . I can't answer that. I've been working for McGregor for the last ten years, and he's *always* been a puzzle to figure out. He never lets anyone come too close to himself or know too much about him. I've also suspected that McGregor's always had something to hide, but up until now, I've never had the guts to see what it is."

"Until now, sir?"

"Maybe, Armstrong, just *maybe* I'll start to look more closely into him after you two finish this assignment." The Asian man got up from his seat, threw the rest of the coffee down the sink, and rinsed out the mug. "Are you ready to go?"

Armstrong glanced down at his half full cup. "Yeah. My hands will start to shake if I drink any more of this stuff; that's probably a good sign that I've had enough for today."

Bridgemohr Apartments, San Francisco, CA
July 17th, 2079, 1408h

Honda dropped the two of them off in front of the duplex; Liszt's first task was to unlock her car that was parked right across from it. It was a luxury sedan made by Hyundai and probably had air-conditioned seats as well as heated ones. As soon as she swept through the car with his magnafone, she closed it back up, and nodded to Armstrong with her approval. "No listening devices or explosives; that's a good sign. Wooster must be slipping up," she commented wryly and handed his magnafone back to him.

"Or maybe he doesn't care?" Armstrong inquired. "Did you carpool to work on purpose yesterday?"

"Naturally; I wasn't about to give Wooster another chance to rid himself of me. Unfortunately for the man who gave me a ride, he chose to open fire at us yesterday, and is now likely being dissected by a medical examiner on a slab in the county morgue." She retrieved a set of keys from her pocket and opened the door with it.

"How often did you two carpool?"

"Every other day," Liszt replied with a shrug. "We split it 50/50."

"Does this mean that if I sit behind the wheel of a car to drive us somewhere, that I might have those same odds of being shot by you?"

"That depends how adventurous your eyes get. And don't you dare suggest that you weren't looking at them again, Tiger."

"No comment," he held up his hands with a chuckle. "Keys? Well, now, that's a bit old school."

"Electronic locks are too easy to hack or fool nowadays. It takes a person with skill to pick one of these; thumb prints and retinal scans are mere child's play to forge." Liszt gestured to the lock with the key before sliding it inside; the bolt slid back without a problem, and she opened the door for them both.

I wonder if killing really does bother her at all. Or maybe she's merely trying to prove that she's good enough to accompany me. Lots of women still think that they have to prove themselves to men these days.

"I'll be back in just a moment," she told him as she headed up a flight up carpeted stairs.

"Need a hand?"

"No thank you," Liszt called back down to him when she reached the top. About two minutes later, she came back down with two full sized suitcases on rolling wheels.

Armstrong's forehead wrinkled as he saw her briefly struggle with them. *Aha. Tough girl; I could have certainly helped her with those. Aw, why the hell don't I?* He climbed up halfway to meet her and took one of them away from her without a word. She gave him a tight-lipped smile in reward, and they made a quick exit from the duplex. Seconds later after they closed the door, she unlocked the car, popped the trunk, and they crossed the street.

She let him load the trunk with both valises, hurried back to the building, and rang the buzzer twice on the outside panel. About ten seconds later, the upper apartment completely burst violently into flames.

Armstrong winced as he noticed a piece of debris nearly hit Liszt on her way back to him and closed the trunk. "Do you leave a path of destruction behind you on an every day basis or what?" he quipped.

"Leaving evidence behind me is just another way for Wooster to track my every movement. Besides, I did a lot of work from home, too." She shrugged, opened the car door, and got inside. He promptly followed suit and secured his seatbelt across his lap and shoulder. Liszt's eyes saw his actions and did the same. "Did you think that I would repeat yesterday's events so soon?"

"Just taking a precautionary measure, like you," Armstrong parried.

"Oh, and just in case you've forgotten, the next thing on our list will be for me to pick up a new magnafone, as well as head to a place that I know of that can add a few helpful apps to it." Before he could open his mouth to argue with her, she revved the engine and took off like a bat out of hell.

"Would now be a bad time to let you know that I really have to go to the little boy's room?"

"I'm sure you'll manage to keep your bladder in check for the next twenty minutes. Even then, I suppose I could pull over onto the side of the road if you absolutely *must* satisfy your urges." She rolled her eyes and brought the car to a rolling stop at the next light, which had just turned green. "Has Honda given you a company credit line on your magnafone, or shall I go about this the usual way with all sorts of strings attached?"

"Lucky you, Harriet, I do. I might need some persuasion, though. He didn't order you to go through me, and I do have a monthly budget to keep." Armstrong rolled his neck from side to side. "Although I might be so inclined to let you use it if you would—"

"Fine." She made a sharp right turn and cut off the car in front of her. The driver proceeded to give her a long but well deserved blare of his horn and the finger. Then she guided the car swiftly over towards the emergency lane onto the highway. "Far be it from me to make you abstain from the call of nature."

He gasped as the seatbelt pressed down on his lap, removed it, and opened the door to extricate himself from the car. Two minutes later after he relieved himself, Armstrong got back in and sighed. "Okay, you can use the credit line."

"Glad you saw things my way. Feeling better now?"

Not my pride, by a long shot.

"Freedom never felt so good," Armstrong declared with an ardent grin.

The rest of the trip over to the magnafone dealer was spent in silence, and just after they walked inside, Armstrong's fingers began to tingle as his phone rang. "I should probably take this," he told her. "Come and get me after you've negotiated a deal. Wait, scratch that. I don't think you're the type to negotiate."

She merely raised her eyebrow at him in response and shuffled over towards a skinny young man with blonde hair who could not have been more than eighteen. "Hello, welcome to Magnafone Mart. Wow, how can I help you out, miss?" The employee's eyes practically fell out of his sockets as he gushed over her with a smile.

Oh, I wish I could actually hear this, Armstrong thought and stepped outside. *She'll have him on his knees in less than two minutes begging her to marry him.*

"Hello, this is Armstrong."

"Nestor? It's Irene. Can you talk, or are you busy?" McGregor's niece asked.

Armstrong turned around to watch the show in front of himself. *Yep. He's trying to maintain his self control. Hey there, bud. Keep those eyes focused upon hers and not down her . . . well, there goes your dignity. She's gonna take advantage of you.*

"No, not busy at all, Irene. I'm just watching some very interesting entertainment at the moment," he returned with a grin.

"Again? Is this like . . . the same kind that you had on last night?"

"Oh, nothing like that. This is rated . . . PG-13. It would have been PG just a moment ago, though, had someone's eyes not popped out of his head." His head tilted to one side as he tried to read what Liszt's mouth was saying. "What can I do for you?"

"Well . . . remember that section of my uncle's house I told you about last night? The forbidden one?" Her speech was very erratic and jittery.

"Yeah, I think so. Why? You didn't—"

"I uh . . . figured out . . . his access code. And I might have . . . um . . . broken in."

"Oh, I admit that as much as that intrigues me, that gives me more than just a bit of concern, Irene. Do you know where your uncle is at the moment?"

"He's still gone, and nobody else knows that I'm down here. But . . . I found some . . . very odd . . . evidence about him . . ." her voice started to tremble.

"Is it bad?"

"Um . . . there are more than five or six different social security cards here. And um . . . multiple birth certificates . . . passports with different names . . .—"

Armstrong remained silent for a moment as he thought. *No surprise there. Just what is he hiding?*

"Uh, Nestor, are you still there?" Irene nervously prodded.

"Yes, Irene, I am, sorry. I was just thinking."

"Okay, and um . . . the most disturbing thing that I found was uh . . . the death certificate."

"Death certificate?"

"Yep. Owen McGregor died in 2001 from . . . mes-o-the-lioma. That sounds familiar, but what *is* that?"

"It's a type of lung cancer." Again, his mind became flooded with all sorts of scenarios that ran through his head. He stopped himself from continuing on and cleared his throat. *She's a civilian, Armstrong. This isn't something she's used to dealing with everyday. Reassure her that everything's going to be all right.*

"What should I do, Nestor?"

"How'd you get this number?"

"I . . . I came across it while I was . . . uh . . . searching . . . as well as somebody . . . uh named Honda. Should I not have done that? Should I call the police?"

"No!" His reply was almost a bark. "Um, I mean, not yet. Vincent Honda is my boss, and he's the head of security for Zionastra. Yes, you should call him and tell him everything that you just told me. Then ask him to pick you up."

I can't risk McGregor or whatever his name is now finding out that she went through his belongings; he might try to kill her.

"Uh, okay."

"You'll be all right, Irene; I'm glad you called me. Now promise me something if you can . . ."

"What is it?"

"Call me back after you've spoken to Honda, okay?"

"I will, Nestor. And . . . thank you."

"I'll be talking to you soon, all right? Don't worry," he whispered the last two words.

"Well, now that . . . I was able to call you, uh, I think I won't," Irene stammered.

"Hey, take a deep breath. Now relax; just think of . . . uh . . . performing that tango with that Argentinian partner of yours. Was he handsome?" His voice became as soft as velvet.

She exhaled very slowly over the line. "Yes, he was."

"Good. How did you feel when you were in his arms?"

"Nervous at first . . . then . . . at home. His eyes were a lot like yours."

She's starting to calm down. That's better.

"Uh-huh, go on," he pressed.

"And . . . I felt safe . . . warm . . . comfortable."

"And when you look at me, what do you feel?"

"I . . . was this supposed to . . .—"

"Relax you, I hope, yes."

"That was . . . working for about . . . ten seconds there," she admitted. "And then it . . . got a little weird."

"Oh, sorry. Sometimes I get a bit full of myself without even realizing it," he chuckled and reached into his pants' pocket as Liszt took a few strides towards him. "You struck a deal already?!"

"I'm sorry?" Irene asked.

"I was talking to Liszt, Irene, sorry. Listen, after you hang up, call Honda. Then call me back right away." Liszt snatched the magnafone from his hand, ran her index finger across the screen, and activated the American Express credit line. She turned the magnafone back around towards him, and after he nodded his approval, she went back inside.

"All right, I'll do that. Talk to you soon, Nestor."

Armstrong went inside the store, and Liszt made a gesture for him to come closer with her fingers as well as her eyes. He obeyed, and she pointed to the kiosk's touch screen with her eyes. He gave her a confused look, and then she turned to give the clerk a flirtatious smile. "I'm sorry, Nick. Apparently, my husband has forgotten how to sign his name." She leaned herself against the counter.

The ex-cop nervously laughed. "Nope, I haven't . . . I just . . . well, honey, did you get the right one? You know how hard I work every day to get you what you want and—"

Liszt batted her eyes at him and mashed her heeled foot upon his very under protected foot, which was only covered by leather. He opened his mouth in pain, but no sound would come out, and the store clerk pulled at his tie nervously. "Really, sir, it's okay. You can just give me your thumb print instead."

Armstrong closed his mouth and clenched his teeth together. "No. I'll sign it. Time of the month again, dear?"

The expression that was upon her face could either be translated to *you are going to get it later on* or *I could just eat you up now.*

He chose to err on the side of caution and produced his John Hancock. "Thank you for shopping at Magnafone Mart. Have a great day." He stepped back nervously away from the counter.

When they got back into her car, he untied his shoe and pulled off his sock to glance at his now red foot. "Goddamn it woman, what the hell was that all about?"

"You apparently needed some direction," Liszt responded coolly and started the engine back up. "You'll live."

"How about a subtle hint next time?" Armstrong lamented and stretched out his now sore foot onto the carpet.

"If I'd been any more subtle, you would have needed *more* direction."

"Now my foot feels like it's on fire. We'd better not have to run anywhere after we talk to this president at Bethesda, or else you're gonna have to drag my ass outta there."

"That's a fair deal." She made a cursory glance down at his throbbing limb. "Sorry. I forgot what kind of shoes I was wearing today . . . or that you were wearing civilian footwear."

He sighed. "I'll be fine in about ten minutes."

"So whom were you flirting with on your phone?"

"Irene."

Listz's foot hit the brakes a little harder than she meant to as they came to a halt for a traffic signal. "I see. What did she want?"

"I was only doing that to calm her down."

"Calm her down?"

"Let me finish before you jump all over me," Armstrong said with a glare.

"Are you doff—jump all over you?" she scoffed. "Not in a hundred years."

"I meant it figuratively, Harriet. Now, she found out that McGregor isn't exactly . . . um . . . McGregor."

"You mean that he lied about his identity?" She hit the accelerator after the light turned green and gave a mock gasp. "How shocking." Her tone was laced with complete sarcasm.

"Yeah. We don't know what his real name is. But the point is that *that* was why I was quote flirting with her. And I don't understand why I have to explain this to you," he groaned and glued his eyes to the road.

I think at this moment that I'd rather be locked in a shed with a ton of dynamite.

"Fine, because I was just thinking that a little silence would be rather lovely right now," she argued but kept her voice civil. "I'll take us next to my acquaintance, who happens to be a private investigator, to get my magnafone updated. I'd ask to scan yours, but I already know which apps I want to be installed, and you may not have the ones I want. Then we'll head to Hope of Bethesda."

He leaned an elbow onto the windowsill.

This is going to be a long drive.

CHAPTER SIX

1 mile from Hope of Bethesda, Sacramento, CA
July 17th, 2079, 1649h

The only stop Liszt made after seeing the private investigator was to refuel her car's very hungry power cells. Recharging cars that ran on electricity literally took moments, as if you were filling up a tank of gas from days in the past. You simply inserted the conductivity rod into your car's capacitor tank, and you were set to run for approximately five hundred miles, depending upon your speed as well as the usual other variables.

While she was doing that, Armstrong had gone inside the convenience store to get himself a red ice Slurpee. He offered to buy her one, too, but she turned him down. "So, do you have a plan of action as to how to make Mr. Franklin talk?" she inquired after he returned.

"That I do, but I've got a question to ask you first," he replied.

"Ask away." Liszt returned the conductivity rod into its charger, taking great care not to get too close to it and hopped back into the car, as did he.

"Have you ever heard of something called the 'placebo' effect?"

"No, but remember that I wasn't born or brought up in this country. Some idioms are still new to me; however, I do know what the word means."

"Well, did you happen to bring any truth serum with you?"

A cruel smile flickered across her face. "If I didn't know any better, Mr. Armstrong, I'd swear that we knew each other in another lifetime."

"I'll take that as a yes, then."

"Correct."

"How do you administer it, through a needle like in the old days?"

"That's generally the accepted practice, yes. Why do you ask?"

He lifted the Slurpee up to his lips and consumed some of it first before giving her his answer. "My little errand into the store was actually to catch two fish with one worm. This drink will work just nicely as a rouse."

"I'm not sure that I follow you."

"I fill up one of your syringes with some of this stuff and tell Franklin that if he won't cooperate with us that we can give him his cancer back. And that it'll kill him within two days." Armstrong pointed to the Slurpee.

"Ah, now you're talking the language I speak rather fluently: extortion."

"However, I'd like to try the word 'please' first, if you don't mind."

"This is your operation; I'll follow your lead, Armstrong."

"But if this does go south, please feel free to unload . . . um . . . Leontine however you'd like. I'll probably have to carry him, so—"

"I'll cover you; it's not a problem."

"And please let me talk to the receptionist inside first."

"You don't think I can speak with that person in a civil manner?"

"What were you saying about following my lead a moment ago, Harriet?" He gently reminded her and gestured to himself as he pulled up to the parking garage just beside the building.

"Of course, you're right," she agreed and rolled down the window to speak with the lot attendant. "Pardon me, my partner and I have an appointment with Mr. Michael Franklin? May we park here, please?" Liszt gave him a trivial smile.

"Sure. Keep these on at all times." The attendant nodded his head, stuck his hand out his window with two clip-on ID badges that very clearly said the word 'VISITOR' on them, and activated the barricade in front of the car. "Just be ready to step through a body scanner and an x-ray machine on your way in."

"Thank you. Any particular place we should park?"

"Third floor. Use the enclosed walkway on the same level to gain access into the building across the street."

"Right." Liszt took the badges and rolled up her window. "This could be a problem. We can't take our guns inside now."

"Well, I did stock up on those smoke bombs and incendiaries before we left the armory. Want to set up some kind of contingency plan in here? I can see . . ." As she brought the car down a row of vehicles, he looked about himself. "Probably about two cameras that make one hundred eighty degree sweeps per row. Not bad."

"I could hack through some of these cars' firewalls and set off some alarms with my magnafone," she offered.

"Ah, park right next to that truck. That'll do nicely." He signaled her attention to a red Nissan truck that could seat probably about six people comfortably. "I brought some sticky tack with me, and I could probably set a few of those smoke bombs on its undercarriage or something."

She obeyed him and parked her car. "So after I set off the car alarms, you'll rush around the back or wherever you end up putting them and set them off?"

"That sounds like a plan B."

Liszt popped the trunk and undid the lock on one of the suitcases with another key. After she opened it, Armstrong came around the back of the car with his backpack. He prepared two smoke bombs, all the while making sure that he crouched down behind a cement support so that the surveillance cameras did not see his actions. She removed a syringe from a white box that was marked with a red cross and slid it into her jacket pocket. "Did you leave your drink inside the car?" she wondered.

"Yep, but before I go fill our needle up with thirty c.c.s of Slurpee, I need you to cover me for a few moments," Armstrong answered her.

"I'm not following you." A hand came rest on one of her hips.

"I need a bit of a distraction for what I'm about to do with the smoke bombs."

"Isit, what do you suggest?"

Tread very carefully, Tiger.

"You're an intelligent, beautiful woman. I'm sure you'll think of something that won't set off any alarm bells or make those sluggish nine to fivers drool too much over you," he announced with a rogue smile.

Her eyes merely met his serenely as she pondered the matter. "You know, I don't know about Zionastra's security staff, but my guards weren't exactly sluggish."

"Those weren't the nine to fivers; that was the swing shift."

"And by having the time to sleep in for a few more hours, that makes them all the better?"

"*Tempus fugit*, Harriet," he chided her with a playful lilt.

"*Ars longa, vita brevis*," she returned with a thoughtful smile. "Very well."

Liszt closed her luggage back up and let him put his knapsack into the back seat. She then proceeded to close the trunk, sauntered towards the front of the red truck they were parked next to, hiked a leg up onto the front bumper, and pretended to adjust the seams of her stockings. She wasn't actually wearing any, but she also made some subtle tweaks to the length of her cream colored skirt and fussed over her shirt.

He set the smoke bombs just underneath the truck's rear bumper, one on either side, and finished just in time to see her undoing one more button than she probably should have. Armstrong cleared his throat to signal her that he had completed his task, and she handed him the needle. "Do you need more time?" she inquired.

"Just a little longer," he quietly responded and ducked back into the car.

Liszt next adjusted the golden necklace that rested around her neck and kissed the tiny little locket that had previously rested next to her heart. He filled up the needle with the red Slurpee about halfway, capped the end with the plastic cover, and pocketed it. After he closed the door, he now observed her preening her hair, closing her eyes, and throwing her head back as she did it. He had to admit now that even he felt distracted.

Moments later, her eyes opened, and she ran one more hand absent-mindedly through her hair. "Ready now?" she asked.

"You could say that," he replied in a non-plussed manner. Armstrong reached for her hand, and she gave him a dubious look. "Didn't you introduce us to the guy there as partners? Or did I misinterpret what you said?"

"Husbands and wives can work together, but it's not necessarily a great idea. We're out of time for another idea, though . . . let's chuck." Without another objection, she slid her fingers through his. Although neither of them meant for the reaction, the touch of their hands was electric.

"You know, this is the second time that you've introduced us as a couple for a cover story today," a flicker of a smirk passed upon his lips as he said this. They began their journey across the walkway, which was about two hundred feet long.

"Would you prefer that I not use it in the future?"

"Well, it's just that . . . oh, never mind." He began to scratch his chin and play with his beard but then stopped his actions once she voice her next question.

"Am I making you nervous?"

Not exactly. Armstrong restrained himself to keep his eyes straight ahead.

"So what do you wanna use for a name?" he asked.

"Oh, you're letting me make the choice, here?"

"A suggestion."

"How about the Parkers? It seems like anything with having to do with Spiderman puts your mind at ease."

"Okay, but not Peter and Mary Jane."

"Robert and Meredith?"

"Sure. Any particular reason why you wanted to use those names?"

"Meredith was my father's name."

"And Robert?"

"Would you prefer something else?"

"No, I just said that . . .—" he sighed. "Never mind."

They strolled over to the building in silence, walked through the security, and one of the guards gave Armstrong a peculiar glance. "What's the needle for, bud?" he inquired.

"Oh, you wouldn't confiscate my husband's insulin, would you? He needs to take it in about ten minutes,"

Liszt laid a hand onto the sentry's arm. "Please, would you allow him to keep it? We'll dispose of it properly, I assure you."

The officer made eye contact with the others; no one gave him any body language or raised a vocal concern. He shrugged. "Fine. Just remember that we've got surveillance all over this place, lady."

"Where might we find Mr. Franklin's office? We've got an appointment to see him," Armstrong inquired.

"Where else do you think? Top floor. The elevators on your right can get you there."

"Thank you."

Both of them went into the lift along with about ten other people. Armstrong let go of her hand and stood just behind her in the back of the elevator to accommodate everyone else. "So about that cover story," he leaned in close to whisper to her. "Are you ever going to elaborate about that?"

As there was very little room for her to do so, she did not turn around. Instead, she motioned to him to come even closer, which he did. "Could you pass for a scientist?"

"Not the stereotypical one, no."

She waited until the elevator stopped onto the next floor, and about four people left. Thankfully, no one came in, and the others separated. "First appearances and impressions are everything, you know."

"True. Are you going to be the one to speak with the receptionist, or am I?"

"I thought you said that you wanted to do that." Now that there was room, Liszt moved away from him and shuffled onto his left hand side. She removed her magnafone from her belt and started to browse the internet for gossip about Franklin.

"I was just double checking that we were on the same page. You practically jumped all over that guard."

One or two pairs of eyes wandered over towards their conversation.

"And if I hadn't done that, what kind of a debacle would we be in now?" She turned to bat her eyelashes at him; hopefully, everyone else would now ignore them and mind their own business. Unfortunately, her actions only increased their attention.

Great. Now I've got to become a full fledged actor, he inwardly groaned.

"You know, we wouldn't be late for our appointment if *you* hadn't set the alarm for p.m., not a.m., sweetheart," Armstrong returned her gentle banter. "Then I could have taken my insulin in the car and not have to bring it—"

Her eyes gave him a deep glare. *Call me that again, and you'll come to regret it.*

Seconds later, she wiped the glare from her face and shrugged. "You're right. It was silly of me to argue like that." She returned her attention to her magnafone.

The rest of the party immediately lost interest in their discussion and left as the elevator stopped at the next floor. After the doors closed, she took a step towards him and straightened his tie. "Next time, don't agree to the husband and wife angle if you don't want me to call you that. I couldn't think of anything else besides that or honey bunch off the top of my head," Armstrong scolded her. "And I knew that saying that would piss you off even more."

"If you had said it, your other foot would be sore now," Liszt remarked and reclaimed her hands. "How's it feel, by the way?"

"Back to normal, I think."

"Right, well, here we are."

After they left the elevator, they traveled to the assistant's bureau. Armstrong chose not to use the same avenue that he tried yesterday and stuck to business. "We'd like to see Mr. Franklin, please."

"Do you have an appointment?" the man inquired.

"It's very urgent that we speak with him; the matter is extremely important."

"I'm sorry, but Mr. Franklin is very busy right now, and unless you have a—"

Armstrong quickly withdrew a fake set of governmental credentials and flashed it at the assistant. "Clear the schedule for now." He put the fraudulent badge and ID back into his pocket.

"Which um . . . I mean, where are you from?"

"FDA. Agent Robert Parker." Armstrong pointed to himself.

"And you?" the secretary demanded of Liszt.

"I'm his partner. We don't have much time." Her eyes narrowed, and she made an impatient huff as she glanced at her watch.

"All right, all right." The assistant held up both hands and touched his fingers to his ear. "Mr. Franklin, sir? Two agents from the FDA are here to see you." Seconds later, the man gave them a polite nod. "Please go right in. Mr. Franklin will be happy to see you now."

When the doors closed behind them, Armstrong withdrew the needle from his pocket, stormed right towards Franklin, and jammed it into his neck. "What the hell? James, get me—"

Liszt held a finger to her lips and shook her head 'no'.

"I wouldn't try to call them if I were you," Armstrong began. His voice was no longer pleasant; he kept the tone civil but ominous. "That serum that I just injected you with has now given you that very nasty disease that you managed to cure yourself of miraculously last year."

"What?!" Franklin roared.

"Yes, we know all about you, and obviously, we're not from the FDA. I can give you the antidote if you come with us and don't make a scene." Armstrong grabbed Franklin by his shirt with both hands and lifted him up from his chair very slightly. "If you do, then I might not be able to find it."

"P—p—please." Franklin's breathing immediately escalated. "I . . . I have a family."

"Wrong," Liszt cut in and disagreed with her head. "Oldest excuse in the book. You *used* to have a family in Seattle until you left them for some other woman last year. Pathetic." Her tongue clicked with dismay on the roof of her mouth.

"What do you want?"

"Your cooperation, for now," Armstrong replied mysteriously and released him. "Now make some kind of excuse to take an early lunch to your assistant and follow us out. You can say that we're putting you under arrest but are not cuffing you because you didn't want to cause a panic."

Franklin's fingers trembled as they touched the spot below his ear. "James? I'll be leaving Bethesda for the rest of the . . . I mean . . . I'm going to be going downtown with these FDA agents. I shouldn't be too long, but just in case, call off the rest of my appointments for the day. No, everything's fine, don't worry. I'll be back to work tomorrow, or at least I should be." His eyes traveled towards his captors, who of course did not reveal any kind of reassurance to him.

"There," Franklin stated and ended the call. "Did I do that all right?"

"Don't try to stall for time; let's go," Armstrong responded coldly and made a motion with his fingers that it was time to leave.

"Who are you people?"

"No questions. Make your way to the door now and act naturally," Liszt hissed.

The president shakily arose from his seat, took a deep inhale, and tried to calmly stroll through the outer office towards the elevator. The assistant watched the entire exchange with a cautious eye. After they filed into the elevator, he swiftly put through a call to security to explain his suspicions.

"So you said that you're not from the FDA. Maybe you're from another fed agency . . . or . . ." Franklin sputtered nervously.

"Don't talk if you're going to get upset and prattle. It'll attract attention to you," Liszt ordered and crossed her arms.

Franklin lowered his head and began to glide one hand over the other.

Armstrong bit his lip. *Wonderful. She's made him even more jittery now.*

"Look, just . . . take a deep breath and relax," he told Franklin. "We just need to take you somewhere so that you can be medically examined."

Liszt's eyes wandered over towards his as if to ask *what are you doing?*

"We'll give you the cure when we get there," the ex-cop went on. "Just do what we tell you, all right?"

"You can answer him," Liszt said.

Their captive stopped rubbing his hands together and wiped them onto his shirt. "Uh, okay, yeah."

When the elevator came to the parking garage access level, it halted instantly. The security officers at the x-ray and body scanners stood up from their positions and removed their weapons. The doors opened, and the three of them found themselves surrounded. "Step away from Mr. Franklin, and come out slowly with your hands up," one guard commanded. He was the same one Liszt had spoken to not ten minutes ago.

"Oh voertsek," Liszt seethed under her breath and glanced at Armstrong. "What are you scheming?"

"Stick to the plan. Do what I do." He seized one of Franklin's arms and linked their elbows together. Liszt followed suit upon Franklin's opposite side. "If they follow us, then go to the contingency."

"Of course," she stated with a nod.

The three of them marched right out in front of the security team. Armstrong eyed them all; no one was carrying anything more dangerous than a zapper. "We're leaving with Mr. Franklin and will return him unharmed to this building in two days," he announced firmly with a clear but authoritative voice. "It'd be best if you all stood down. We'd rather not have to make things get ugly here."

"Kidnapping a person makes things ugly, bud."

No one obeyed Armstrong. He shook his head, heaved a heavy sigh, and quickened the trio's pace towards the covered walkway.

"Hold it, or else we'll—" the guard began to say as Armstrong passed him. He was about to fire until Armstrong's elbow sailed into his chin.

"Okay, plan B!" he yelled. Moments later, Liszt broke herself away from them, and pulled her magnafone off of her skirt's belt. Armstrong still held Franklin and yanked him down the hallway. She also joined their sprint and quickly slid her fingers across the LCD touch screen.

Three seconds later, she successfully completed her duty. Several car alarms started to blare throughout it; about five seconds later, they reached the garage, and made it to the car. "Get this thing open, him inside, and ready to go," Armstrong commanded her.

She did as told, unlocked the car, shoved Franklin in the back seat, and started the engine. Armstrong ran around to the truck next to them, activated the smoke bombs, and threw open the passenger door.

Unfortunately, Bethesda's security officers had followed them and opened fire with their zappers. The ex-cop rolled underneath the door for protection while Franklin just cowered in the back seat. "Hey you, make yourself useful," he barked. "Gimme my backpack."

The president slid down in his seat and covered his head as well as his ears. Liszt thankfully had not strapped herself in; she leaned over and did as Armstrong wanted.

"Thanks. Put your seatbelt on, Franklin. You're no good to us dead."

Armstrong dug into the backpack, quickly located a white blarney, and lobbed it at the guards who dared to venture even closer to them. He tossed out another one for good measure, then hopped into the car, and Liszt took off without another moment to lose.

"Oh my god, oh my god, oh my god," Franklin repeated this mantra to himself and closed his eyes.

"Put your damn seatbelt on, Franklin!" Armstrong yelled.

Franklin finally obeyed him but continued to whimper.

Liszt wildly drove the car through the garage; the lot attendants had the barrier down as she approached the exit. "So, how good is this bumper?" Armstrong inquired.

"Don't know. Let's find out," she announced with half a smile and continued forward with some more acceleration.

The barrier collided with her bumper and made a slight dent; it did not slow them down as much as Armstrong thought that it would. Franklin cried out in terror after their car made contact with it, and he looked at Liszt. "Is he going to distract you?"

"If he's going to scream loudly like that for the next four hours, yes," she responded icily.

Armstrong shrugged, leaned back, and knocked Franklin out. "I couldn't take the chance, now, could I?"

"So, I thought that you said that you were just going to threaten him with the the syringe." She slowed their speed to a legal limit.

"I was getting hungry and didn't want to fool around."

"Want to make a stop now for food before we leave Sacramento or later on?"

"Now. We'll pick up something for him just in case he wakes up before we get back." Armstrong pointed to Franklin with his thumb and put on his seatbelt.

"By the way, nice bluff back there. I was thinking that you were going to whip out an old badge from your police days."

"I thought about it but decided against doing so because I figured that someone was probably going to try and get in touch with SFPD. Then we'd be sitting ducks; besides, people seem to have a bit more reverence for federal authority than they do local," Armstrong pulled his tie away from his neck.

"So you were a homicide detective?"

His head snapped towards hers. "How did you—"

"I did some research on you, remember?" Her eyes met his for a fleeting moment then went immediately back to the road to concentrate. "You're still on friendly terms with one or two people, I believe."

"Does this info come from your private dick back home?"

"Perhaps."

"What else does he know about me?"

"Just the officers' names, nothing more."

"I know that you didn't trust me very much yesterday, but how about now?"

"Like respect, trust is earned. I don't give it out freely, and from the look of it, neither do you." She removed one hand from the wheel and set her elbow on the rest in between them. "But I trust you more than I do your boss, especially now. What about you?"

"Are you asking me if I trust you more than I trust my boss?"

"To put it bluntly, yes."

"I can't answer that yet." He pulled the tie down even more and undid his top button.

"How can you *still* believe that McGregor isn't running this whole operation to get this cure for himself? Your own superior Honda could even be a part of this agenda, too, and just be pulling the wool over your eyes."

He sighed, leaned his face upon his hand, and rested his elbow against the windowsill. "I don't know."

"Well, you've got a few hours to make up your mind, then."

"Look, I just don't know what to believe. I've worked with Honda for three years now; I've barely known *you* for a day."

"I realize that, and I'm not trying to rush you into this," her voice softened. "I had two months to make up my own damn mind after I found that burner. But it may come down to having to pick a side soon."

"What do you want from me, then, an apology?"

"No. But if I find out that your immediate superior is putting up a façade, then there's no question in my mind of what I'll do. All I ask is that you give this matter some careful consideration, and I'm sorry that you don't have more time to sort this out. If I could, I'd give you the same amount of time that I had."

Armstrong remained taciturn for the next fifteen seconds as he ran a hand through his hair and pondered his predicament.

"If Honda can't be trusted, then we need to get to Irene first," he finally stated.

"Agreed. I can take Franklin over to your armorer, what's his name . . . Nathan? And you can meet Honda at McGregor's house. Want me to drop you off there first?"

"Yeah, thanks." His stomach angrily howled at him. "Can we stop for dinner soon?"

"Very well. I am feeling rather peckish myself," she agreed, slowed the car down, and made a turn into a driveway of a fast food restaurant.

"So uh, can I ask you something personal?"

After she guided the car into the drive-thru lane and stopped behind a short line of cars, Liszt turned her head to give him her attention. "I'll let you know if it's inappropriate."

"Before we went inside Bethesda, I saw you kiss something upon your neck. Is that a locket?" Armstrong gestured to her heart.

"It is." For a moment, it seemed like Liszt was not going to continue; her fingers instinctively went towards her chest and toyed with the jewelry. "It's a photograph of my father Meredith."

When she failed to expound upon the subject, he decided not to press it, and peered at the fast food restaurant's three dimensionally projected menu. Surprisingly, though, she did go on. "He died just shortly after my fifteenth birthday; the locket was a present from the year before. I had the picture put there years later; it was empty when he gave it to me."

"I didn't think that people still wore those; I'm a bit surprised that you would," Armstrong commented.

"Earlier today, you mentioned the fact that you were taught to shoot by a Native American tribal chief, yes?"

"Adam Lynch," he said with a nod. "I haven't seen him in at least five years now."

"What kind of gun did he teach you to shoot with?"

"We started with small rifles and pistols when I was about ten. Then as my skills improved, he allowed me to shoot with bigger guns. Let's see here." He tapped his chin pensively. "My first gun was actually an air rifle with spring action loading. Then . . . a Smith and Wesson M&P .40. It doesn't look too different than that tranquilizer gun that I was using, actually."

"No Colt pistols?"

"Oh, the cowboy six shooter came much later. Those things pack one helluva punch for recoil, lemme tell you. Have you ever fired one of those suckers?"

She inched the car forward as traffic slowly moved. "No."

"I've got one at home; you should try it sometime. Well, I mean that if . . . if we ever get a spare moment to ourselves," he said with a shrug.   .

"Would that qualify as a second date?"

Armstrong completely undid his tie and let it hang around his neck. "You're on, but remember, you're the one who's been calling them dates, not me."

"I."

"What?"

"You're using incorrect grammar; the correct word to use would be I, not me. I was the one who had been calling them dates."

"And you're *still* doing it." Armstrong gave her a smug grin.

She gave him an exasperated sigh, and the corners of her mouth went upward towards a smile. "You knew that I'd do that?"

"And you fell for it, too." He reached into his pocket for his magnafone.

"Arrogant bastard."

"Then let this arrogant bastard buy you dinner." He passed it over to her.

"You know, I think that it's about time that we finally used that twenty dollar bill that one of your friends so kindly handed over to you yesterday." She withdrew the denomination from a small strongbox that was hidden in the console located in between them.

"Well, either way, dinner's on me, I guess."

"You know just how to pamper a woman, don't you?" She handed the magnafone back to him with a smirk.

"My day just isn't complete without fulfilling her every single whim."

CHAPTER SEVEN

Zionastra Medical Center
July 17th, 2079, 2128h

"Get your goddamned hands off of me!" Franklin screamed and struggled with Nathan Falk and Liszt. "I'm not going into that thing!"

"It's an open body scanner, Mr. Franklin. We won't hurt you," Falk tried to placate him.

"The more you struggle, the more difficult this is going to be," Liszt spat.

"You stuck a goddamned needle into my neck and gave me—"

"Red dye number four and corn syrup? That's hardly lethal," she finished for him. Franklin glared bitterly, got one hand free from her, and elbowed Falk in the ribs with it.

The Irishman momentarily lost his grip and doubled over. Instead of running away, Franklin went straight for Liszt's neck. He wrapped his fingers around her throat and started to strangle her air passages. "I must obey. You are interfering," he whispered to her. "I must obey."

Falk arose, removed a syringe from his pocket, and jammed it into Franklin's neck. As he became distracted, his fingers loosened themselves from around her neck, and he fell onto the ground. Falk threw the needle away in the nearby medical waste bin and scratched his head as he tried to comprehend what Franklin meant.

Liszt took shallow breaths as she regained her composure and joined Falk at his side. "What the hell do you think he meant by that?" he wondered. "He said something about us interfering. Interfering with what?"

"I'm not sure," she wheezed. "Should . . . get him in the . . . machine."

"Aye, that's a good idea, I'll boot it up. Would you like some oxygen in the meanwhile, Miss Liszt?"

She shook her head 'no'; he journeyed over to the controls and did so. About a minute later after she caught her breath, Liszt helped Falk carry Franklin over to the machine and heave him onto the electronic gurney. They returned to the scanner operations terminal, and Falk initiated its process. "Hmm . . . that's just as I thought," he declared and stroked his chin thoughtfully.

"No cancer cells, right?"

"Indeed, Miss Liszt." Something else, however, on the monitor caught his eye. "Wait a moment, now."

"Find something else?"

"An anomaly of sorts, yes."

"What is it?"

Falk zoomed the camera lens in and squinted his eyes upon the images. "There are things that are attached to every single cell I see here, like nanites. But I'm not sure that I could identify them as such."

"What do they resemble?"

"Well, like I said, Miss Liszt, they appear to look like nanites. Maybe they *are* nanites of some sort, but I don't think that Sondheim could have fabricated anything like these. Medical technology is amazing these days, but . . .—"

"But," she pressed him.

"But I don't know what the hell these things are! And that frustrates me." Falk pounded his fist onto the console.

"Could you do some backwards engineering to reverse this cure and find out what they do?"

"I could, but I'm afraid that the tools that I have might damage or break these buggers. If you don't know what you're doing with nanotechnology, bad things can happen. Who knows if these little machines have got safeguards built into them to trigger some kind of defensive response if somebody tampers with 'em?"

"Do you think that they self-replicate along with the cells? New cells are being made all the time in the body, right?"

"Aye, they are. I could take a blood sample from him and find out," Falk agreed.

"You know, when we first kidnapped him, he didn't seem to give us too much trouble. Perhaps that was because he was scared; he thought he was going to die. But when I said that what we gave him wasn't lethal—"

"He attacked you. Mmm, this is very interesting indeed. He went into self preservation mode, and instead of choosing to flee, he chose to fight. This suggests that something electrical occurred inside of him, like a switch flicking on or something."

"The issue that perplexes me most is what he said while he was attempting to choke me to death," Liszt remarked and brushed some of her hair behind her ears. "I must obey. I know that it's possible to brainwash someone using propaganda, sleep deprivation, and psychology, but is it feasible using . . . those things?"

"I don't say this often, Miss Liszt, but I think that the sky might be limit here. If these machines are actually doing that, can we remove them? And if we're able to do so, would that bring the cancer back?"

Liszt arose from the chair she'd been sitting on and gave Falk a very pointed stare. "Before we go on here, Mr. Falk, there's something I must know."

Falk shut the body scanner console down and crossed one leg over the other. "Speak your mind, Miss Liszt."

"How well do you know your employer?"

"McGregor, you mean? I've been here at Zionastra from the beginning. He hired me himself, you know." He pointed his thumb towards himself. "Let me see; we've been around for about seventeen years now. And Sondheim Incorporated started about the same time. The rivalry that's been going on between the two of us was long before they got the cure for cancer, that's for sure."

"Do you think that McGregor's only interested in this cure for himself, or does he truly want to bring Sondheim down?"

"Well, I don't think Sondheim's done anything really wrong here. His overall goal is admirable, and he achieved it. I think that he might have taken some shortcuts to get to it, but I can't really pinpoint as to how he did it . . .—"

"I'd like an answer to my question, Falk." She crossed her arms defiantly. "If you're a part of any sort of plan to steal this cure, consider yourself upon Leontine's to do list, with an up close and personal chat."

"My, you've got quite an imagination there, Miss Liszt."

"It's not very difficult to keep one when you're on the run and have to constantly think one step ahead of your enemy." Her eyes narrowed. "And I *always* come prepared." Liszt's hand went behind her back to place her hand on the grip of her regular semi-automatic pistol.

"Now just what kind of bloody gratitude is that? First of all, you threaten me with the gun that I created just for you, and now you won't even use it on me? What kind of half-wit logic is that, woman?" His hands moved to his hips.

"Enough, Falk, it's time for you to make a choice. You're either for me or against me; there is no middle ground here," Liszt snarled, withdrew the gun, and trained it upon him.

He shook his head 'no'. "I'm not taking anyone's side here, not until I find out what's going on in this man's body. But I'll tell you the truth, Miss Liszt, I don't know what McGregor's plans are. And if they do happen to entail him getting the cure for his own selfish purposes, this old man has no intention of being a part of that plan. Especially if this cure really *does* have that awful side effect. I'd rather die of that disease first rather than lose my brain to that. There," he sighed and removed his hands from his hips. "Does that answer your question now?"

She eyed him carefully for another fifteen seconds; her face remained a calm but professional mask. Finally, she put the gun away. "Yes, you've been as clear as a bell. Thank you."

"Good, now back to work for me. And it's time to also bring in the cavalry."

"What do you mean?"

"Well, dearie, it's nearly ten in the evening. I have a staff that can work 'round the clock doing what's needed to be done."

"Don't bring in anyone you can't absolutely trust; I recommend limiting your support staff to two people *only*," she held up her thumb and index finger.

"How much do you know about medical science, missy?"

"My knowledge is pretty average, really. It's probably no more than what Armstrong knows," she shrugged.

"So how many people would you bring along with you in a firefight?"

"What a peculiar question."

"Humor me; I'm a peculiar man, Miss Liszt." He pointed to himself again and walked over to Franklin's body. She followed him into the next room.

"Three people, myself included."

"Exactly. And if there are only two people working on this after I leave, then it won't be enough, will it?"

"Why would you leave?"

"Contrary to what you might see in the movies, there are people who actually get a good night's rest from day to day. That's precisely what I'm aiming to do in about an hour. Now if you'll excuse me, I've got a few phone calls to make now." He shooed her out of the infirmary, and she huffed impatiently at him.

"I suppose I'll go get a room for the night for myself," she muttered.

"A room? Don't you live in the city?"

"I used to, but I had to well . . . incinerate my abode."

When he gave her an odd look, she rolled her eyes. "It's a long story."

"Don't bother to explain it. We've got some cots here if you'd like, down in the armory. It's not like sleeping on a bed of feathers, but you're welcome to one."

"Thank you; I might take you up on that offer."

McGregor Mansion, Palo Alto, CA
July 17th, 2079, 2157h

Alarms went off in Armstrong's head as he traveled up the steps to the mansion and rang the door bell. No one answered it; he gingerly tested the doorknob and found that it was unlocked. There were some lights on in the house, but there was no outward sign of life, and that made him extremely nervous. Armstrong's hand instinctively pulled the luke off of his backpack's gun rack and unfolded it as quietly as he possibly could. When the gun was ready for action, he turned the knob fully, and shoved it open with the muzzle of the luke.

Armstrong had long since changed into his Spidey suit; he had packed away his formal wear into Liszt's trunk. He now let the goggles that had been resting upon the top of his head fall onto his eyes and activated the infrared scanner as he slowly edged his way through the house. The unfortunate drawback from wearing those goggles was that he now had no peripheral vision whatsoever; he had to rely upon his ears for that.

Perspiration began to settle on the back of his neck now; the house was by no means hot. His phone tingled his fingers as it quietly rang and made him flinch backward slightly. "Armstrong," he whispered.

"Nestor? It's Irene. Mr. Honda's here with me, and we see that you're in the house. Come towards the study, and you'll see where this secret passage is."

"Are you all right?"

"I'm okay, thanks. Mr. Honda got here about an hour ago."

"Why's the house so empty? Where's Lester?"

"It's his day off. That's kind of the reason why I picked today to be nosey. The only person on staff that's working here is the cook, and he's out shopping. Oh, and the gardener might also be on property, but I'm not sure. He lives in a cottage about an acre away from the mansion."

Armstrong lowered his weapon and walked towards the study. "Are you behind the grandfather clock? I notice that it's moved from where I saw it last night."

"Yeah. There's a staircase there, too. Just follow the light. Thanks for coming, by the way."

"I'll be right there," he assured her.

Two minutes later, Armstrong found Honda and Irene. She appeared to be calm, as did Honda, which was no surprise. The Asian man was leaning over the table littered with the evidence that she had found and taking pictures of it all with his magnafone when Armstrong strolled inside the chamber.

Irene instantly hurried over to Armstrong and gave him a warm hug with both arms around his neck. He winced at her strong grip but then accepted the embrace and patted her on the back with his free hand. The other still kept his luke handy, just in case.

When she pulled away, she gave him a perplexed look. "What's with the gun?"

"Well, the house *was* empty, and the door was unlocked. Remember that I used to be a cop, Irene?"

She lightly smacked her forehead. "Oh, right. I totally forgot, sorry."

"So did you call the police?" Armstrong gently prodded her.

"No, you told me not to, and Mr. Honda agreed with me," Irene said and wrinkled her forehead.

"Good. We don't need the complication." Armstrong strolled over to the other side of the table where Honda stood.

Honda shoved some miscellaneous pieces of paper away from himself and continued to take several photographs of the forged paperwork. "Why didn't you give me a call before you came over, Armstrong?" he inquired without glancing upward.

"It was a last minute decision, sir. Liszt offered to drop me off here; she took Michael Franklin over to Falk. When he finds something, she'll give me a call."

"Was he hurt?"

"No; he didn't put up too much of a fight when we got him out of Bethesda."

"Oh, how'd you manage that?"

"I stuck 30 c.c.s of red Slurpee into his throat and told him that if he didn't come with us, that he'd die of cancer in two days."

"Good thinking. Sometimes idle threats don't work," Honda said with a short chuckle. "No property damage, then?"

"Well, we might have taken out a parking garage barrier during our flight. But that's all, I swear." Armstrong held up two fingers. "Scout's honor."

"Sounds minimal, then. Well done, Armstrong." Honda finally gave his subordinate his attention. "Did you get the name of the mineral company that Bethesda is tied to?"

"No, but I'm sure that that information won't be too hard to come by. Like most CEOs, he was very arrogant when we were in his territory. But once I shoved the needle into his neck, it was all too easy after that."

"So you walked right into his office and did it right off the bat?"

"Pretty much," Armstrong replied noncommittally.

"You were hungry, weren't you?"

Armstrong let out a hearty laugh and relaxed a bit more. "Yes, sir, I was."

Don't let down your guard too much, Tiger. Remember, he could be working for the boss, Liszt's voice chided him.

"Mr. Honda, did you know about any of this?" Armstrong finally asked.

Honda's dark eyes pierced through Armstrong's as he tried to gauge what his employee was inferring. Five seconds later, he gave his answer. "No. I came as quickly as I could after Miss McGregor phoned me."

Armstrong's eyes wandered over toward Irene, and she confirmed Honda's story with a nod. "He got here about half an hour after I did so," she told him.

"Without sounding disrespectful, Mr. Honda, I need to know something else."

"And what would that be?"

"Where do you stand with Mr. McGregor?"

Honda stopped his previous activities, put away his magnafone, and leaned onto the table in front of him. "McGregor has been good to me all these years, Armstrong. He's always come close to skirting the law but never has directly broken it, well, until now, that is. I've never known him to be anything but power hungry and ruthless."

"If his real name isn't McGregor, then what is it? Have you found anything in here that could tell us?" Armstrong demanded.

"All of these fingerprints, retinal scans, and dental records have been swapped out with this Owen McGregor who passed away in 2001. We need someone with federal credentials to trust; it's too big for me to handle all by myself," Honda explained.

"Um, I'm sorry to interrupt you, but I've got a rehearsal to get to in the next hour," Irene said politely and pointed to her watch. "If I miss it, then I get cut from the show, and I *just* made the audition yesterday." She paused to glance at Armstrong. "That's kind of the reason why I was so cheery when I met you. I'd just gotten a text message about five minutes before that confirmed it."

"Congratulations," Armstrong nodded. "But that's pretty strict."

"That's show biz," she shrugged.

"I'm sorry, but I don't think that you should go."

"Excuse me?" Irene's face became a question mark, and her foot started to tap onto the ground impatiently.

"That's a bit extreme, Armstrong," Honda remarked. "I can drive her to her rehearsal and make sure that she gets there safely. You can head back to the lab and check in on Franklin as well as Liszt."

"You haven't answered my question, sir," Armstrong eyed the man warily. "This is some pretty damning evidence against the boss." He made a motion towards the table with his rifle.

"I don't like what you're implying, Armstrong." Honda's hands went behind his back, and suddenly, Armstrong raised the rifle instinctively.

"And I don't like what's going on here. Give me an answer." The ex-cop's tone darkened but did not raise in volume.

"Lower your weapon now."

"It's not going to happen."

"Are you prepared to kill me? Remember what that gun can do at this distance."

Armstrong backed away so that he was closer to the stairs. "Tell me whose side you are on . . . mine . . . or McGregor's. *Now.*"

"How can you point a gun at me like this, Nestor? After all I've done for you in the past three years . . ." Honda took a step forward towards him, but Armstrong's finger came closer to the trigger.

"You won't give me a straight answer about McGregor. How in the hell can I trust you now?"

The Asian man glanced at Irene who was literally trembling. "Please leave the room now, Miss McGregor. I don't want you to get hurt."

Irene nodded, started towards the stairs, and Armstrong suddenly grabbed her arm. She screamed out in surprise, and he fired his gun at Honda. A green field encompassed Honda's body, and the charges all bounced off of him. Moments later, Honda snapped his fingers, and the entire room burst into flame.

Armstrong tried again to unload some more shots, but the more he did, the faster they hit Honda's shield and fed the already hungry fire. "Crap," he muttered.

What in God's name is he doing? I've never seen anyone do that before!

He attempted to block Honda's exit but to no avail. The Asian man lifted his hand slightly, and Armstrong fell back a few feet against a wall that was already burning. Armstrong cried out from the pain as the fire started to melt through the layers of the protective suit and threw himself onto the floor to roll around and put it out.

Two seconds later, Honda climbed up the stairs and was gone from sight.

Armstrong picked himself up from the floor. "Damnit! The evidence; we've got to save it before it . . . hurry, Irene!"

She just froze in place and watched with terror as the flames quickly began to engulf the secret passageway. He seized her with both hands and forced her to look into his eyes. "I know you're scared, but I won't let anything happen to you. Now help me before this whole place starts to come down on us."

"Okay," she nodded and started to grab as many pieces of paper as she could.

The fire had not yet spread to the table, but it was coming close. Armstrong whirled around so that his back was to her. "Unzip my backpack and throw what you can in here." Irene did as told; he also snatched what he could from the table with one hand and quickly handed the papers off to her. Both of them now were sweating profusely and began to cough. "Okay, zip me back up, and let's get outta here."

Armstrong closed his eyes briefly and dialed 911. "911, what is your emergency?" an operator serenely inquired.

"There's a fire at . . . where the hell are we?" he snapped at Irene after she had just followed his instructions.

"17 Oakland Boulevard," she said with a cough.

He repeated the address, grabbed her hand, and yanked the both of them up the stairs. "Is everyone out of the residence?" the operator asked.

As they ran up the passage, he answered her in between labored breaths. "We're . . . just going . . . outside now."

"Will you need an ambulance?"

"No. But we've got some . . . smoke inhalation here," he wheezed. "Just some O2."

"The fire department is on the way, sir. Stay calm."

Ten minutes later, the Palo Alto Fire Department arrived, quenched the fire, and issued some oxygen to both Irene as well as Armstrong. The captain approached him first. "Any idea how this started?" he inquired.

"Not sure." Armstrong accepted the facial mask from Irene, took a few breaths, and then handed it back to her. "One minute, we were looking over some important documents, and the next thing we knew, we saw sparks coming from an outlet. I rushed to go find the breaker box, but since I don't live here, I couldn't find it. I went back downstairs to get her, and we saved what we could. That's why . . ." he coughed.

Irene gave him the mask again and remained silent.

"That's why you needed the oxygen," the captain stated. "Well, you should have just gotten the hell outta dodge." He glanced at the luke. "What kind of weapon is that?"

"It's an assault rifle, and I'm licensed to carry one. Besides, it's non-lethal."

"Okay, okay, relax." The man held up his hands. "I'm no cop."

"Captain McCully?" One of his colleagues approached their group. "We'll have to wait until the inspector makes his call, but I'm pretty sure that the fire was electrical. Thankfully, this house is made out of some damned thick concrete and quality wood."

"Thanks, Lieutenant," McCully returned. He placed his hands onto his hips to oversee his crew's clean up of their equipment and noticed Irene shivering. "I've got a blanket in the truck, miss. Need one?"

"I think I'll . . . I'll be okay." Her hands rose to her sides, and Armstrong shoved the mask back into the captain's hands. He opened the cab's rear door, jumped onto the truck's step, took a blanket out from underneath the seat, and placed it around her shoulders. "Thank you."

"Just how in the hell did you know where—"

"I used to be a cop," Armstrong interrupted him. "SFPD."

"Well, that explains it. All right, well, lucky you, miss, you might be able to still live here. But don't go back inside until our inspector puts a little note on your door saying that it's okay to enter. Oh, and you might wanna call your insurance company in the morning, too," the captain told them and cleared his throat to double the volume of his voice. "Local six, let's GTFO."

After they had gone, Armstrong turned towards her. "Do you own a car?"

"Yeah, but . . . I don't think that I . . . well . . .—" She was still shaking.

"Then I'll drive."

"Where are we going?"

"Back to my place. You can't stay here, and honest to God, I need another shower. I feel like hell," he sighed.

"Can we start your car with your magnafone? Or did you leave it inside?"

"No, I've got it." Irene reached into her pocket, pulled it out, but the device slipped out of her hands onto the ground. "Damnit." She bent down to retrieve it as did he, and their hands met upon the magnafone.

He let go first and put his gun away onto the backpack's gun rack. "Do you drink?"

"Not very much, no. But I think . . . I may need something to help me sleep."

"Well if you don't like what I've got back at my place, I've got some mickeys that I could give ya." He motioned with his head to her that they should be on their way. "I'm sorry about your rehearsal; I realize what that must have meant to you, Irene. Did you have a big part?"

"No, but now it means that I'll have to start from square one again and go audition somewhere else," she sighed and made one last cough.

"I'd wait to do that until we know for sure that your uncle doesn't want to kill you. Everything's so up in the air right now that . . . well . . . now I'm not even sure if I still work for Zionastra." *Yeah, that was a good one. Pull a gun on your boss. You'll be lucky if you can go back and clean out your own office.*

"Yeah, no joke. Why didn't you trust him? He seemed like a decent guy."

"Unlock the car, and we'll talk on the way, all right?" Armstrong pointed to the vehicle that was in front of them. "This belongs to you, right?"

"Yeah. I hope it doesn't get blown up like one of those spy movies; I just finished making the last payment for this last month," she sighed and obeyed him.

"I'll do my best to make sure that it won't happen." They entered the car, and Armstrong started the engine. "Here's what I know so far, Irene."

After he shared the whole web of intrigue for the next hour, her eyes widened with complete surprise. "I guess I'd better stay with you, then," she agreed and leaned back against the headrest.

Armstrong nodded. "I can hardly believe it all myself. If I hadn't experienced these last two days myself, I would have locked whoever was telling this fantastic story up in the loony bin and tossed away the key." He lifted one of his hands away from the steering wheel into the air. "If that weren't crazy enough, now my immediate boss has got some kind of new or foreign technology that I've never seen before! What in sam hell is going on, Irene?"

She sighed. "I don't know, but I think that I'd rather be reading about it than be stuck in the middle of this. Do you think this would make a good movie?"

Both of his hands gripped the wheel even more tightly now than before. "Leave it to you to think about the world of entertainment at a time like this."

"It's how I deal with stress, Nestor. Take it or leave it," Irene glowered.

"Sorry. I make jokes too, and it was wrong of me to deflect my anger towards you."

She ran her fingers back through her hair. "I shouldn't have snapped at you. I'm the one who should be sorry."

Both of them spent the rest of the ride to his apartment in silence.

CHAPTER EIGHT

Dienes Villa, San Francisco, CA
July 18th, 2079, 0642h

Armstrong woke up to the smell of freshly brewed coffee in his apartment, slipped a t-shirt over his head, and padded into his bathroom in his boxers. He had not slept very well at all; he spent about half of the night tossing and turning. The previous night had been filled with a dream about taking a boat ride somewhere. When he had woken up from that one, at least he wasn't bathed in sweat.

After relieving himself from the call of nature, he slowly trudged into the kitchen to find Irene already up and scouring his cupboards. "Morning," she greeted him. Her salutation was not nearly as perky as it had been yesterday.

"Can I help you find something?" he asked with a yawn. "I'm afraid I don't have any of that mate stuff you drink."

"That's okay, I just found some tea bags near your stove. A mug, maybe?"

"Oh, just to your left and above your head. Grab me one, too, please."

Irene did as he asked and filled her mug with some water from the tap. She placed hers into the microwave and yawned herself; she watched him serve himself some coffee by pressing down on a plastic tab. "Thanks for making this, by the way. Hope it wasn't too hard to figure out. I thought for sure that I'd be waking up earlier than you," he told her.

"How fast did those drugs hit me?"

"Like I thought. You were a goner in about thirty seconds."

"Oh, well, I'm glad I was so easy," she chuckled and looked at the microwave's spinning tray. "You could probably slip those into anything I consume now. Maybe I should keep an eye on you, too."

He lifted the mug up to his lips and glanced at the coffee machine's clock. "I think I went to bed at about eleven thirty. You hit the sack fifteen minutes before that; did you just wake up now?"

"Five minutes before you, I think." Irene rubbed her eyes groggily, and the microwave finally finished heating the water. She set a tea bag into it and leaned against the counter. "So, what can I make for you this morning?"

"Make for me? Shouldn't I be saying that to you?" Armstrong took another sip of coffee and hummed happily as it slid down his throat.

"Well, I'm still upset . . .—"

"That makes sense."

"And there are very few things that can actually relax me. Cooking is one of them."

"What about dancing?"

She smiled and began to dip the bag in and out of the mug. "I love doing it, but sometimes, it isn't very relaxing."

"So when is it?"

"When is it what?"

"When is it relaxing?"

"You didn't answer my original question," Irene reminded him gently.

"I think I've lost track already; I'm not very good with mornings." He yawned again and scratched his day old stubble. "What was it?"

"What would you like for breakfast?" she laughed.

"Oh. I dunno . . . surprise me."

"But I don't know what you like and don't like! I don't even know what you have to eat, which is why I—"

"I hate oatmeal and love bacon. That's it."

"Really? That's it?"

"But I don't think I have any bacon," he said with a frown. "I don't think I have any low-fat stuff, sorry."

"Why would you think that I—oh, how typical," she groaned and clucked her tongue against the roof of her mouth. "Look, just because I'm a dancer, it doesn't mean that I don't like to eat or love low fat food! It takes a lot of damn hard work to look like this!" Irene hit her palm onto the counter top. "Should I start asking you if your cupboards are stocked from here to Nevada with doughnuts because you used to be a cop?"

"I don't doubt it. Sorry." *You learn something new every day.*

She sighed angrily and rolled her eyes. "That's all right. I just get so sick of the assholes who look at me like I'm some kind of nut job when I'm at McDonald's eating a big mac with some fries. *Then* I get the people who come by and say 'oh honey, should you be eating that'? That's after they find out what I do for a living."

"So how do you really feel about that, Irene?" he joked.

Irene laughed in spite of herself and removed the tea bag from her mug. "Forget about it and tell me what you want to eat before you get a bowl of cold, wet, soggy oatmeal, you turd."

"Honestly, I'll settle for a hard boiled egg and maybe some toast. How does that sound to you? What would *you* like?"

"That sounds fine to me. Now, where are your sauce pans?"

"Below the stove . . . somewhere." Armstrong nudged the drawer with his foot.

"Great! I see that some of your cooking utensils are already out here, so that answers my next question. So out you go." She shoved him out of the kitchen. "A woman needs space to work."

"For two hard boiled eggs, really? All you do is just watch the water boil for the first ten minutes," he lamented.

Irene took the pan out from underneath the stove and raised it above her head. "This could very well pass as a blunt instrument, couldn't it?"

"Think I'll go take a shower now." Armstrong set his mug down and pointed down his hallway to his bathroom.

"Good answer," she called after him.

Twenty minutes later after he took his shower and ran a razor over himself, he dressed in a t-shirt with an SFPD logo on it and a pair of sweat pants. Armstrong approached the kitchen carefully with his now lukewarm mug of coffee. "Uh, would it be okay with you if I heated this up in the—"

An arm shot out of the kitchen, grabbed the coffee, and set it down near the microwave.

"Thanks."

"The eggs are nearly done; I'm just toasting the bread now. Hope you like yours pretty well done," Irene told him.

"As long as it's not black, you're good. On the reservation, there was this one lady that I lived with once that used to use one of those old fashioned toasting ovens, you know, with the rack and everything. The only problem was with it was that you had to watch the toast, and she rarely did. About ninety percent of the pieces of toast I ate while I was under her roof were charred on one side only."

The microwave went on about ten seconds later. "So since I conked out like a log last night, how did you sleep?

"Just fine," he lied. "I scooped you off of the couch and put you into the bedroom. Then I fell asleep next to you about fifteen minutes later, like I said."

"Look, I hope that this isn't too inconvenient for you, but since I slept in my clothes last night . . . um . . . I was wondering—"

"You're like a four or something, right? That's what they say . . . for women's clothing sizes?"

As she came back out of the kitchen with his coffee, her jaw dropped. "How did you . . ." Then her eyes narrowed. "Congratulations, then, are in order, I guess. I didn't feel a thing." Her jaw firmly closed itself shut; it then quivered back and forth spasmodically. "Did ya get to take note of my cup size, too? Or are you the type to just . . . do some hands on investigation?"

"What? No, I just took a glance at the label in your shirt, that's all!" He nearly spilled the hot coffee onto himself. "I may be a cocky bastard, but I've *never* taken advantage of a drugged or drunk woman. A tipsy woman, maybe, but never a drunk one."

She had desperately been trying to keep a straight face, but it was too hard. Three seconds later, she broke out into uncontrollable laughter. "Oh, I *so* had you," she said in between breaths and leaned onto the counter as she tried to keep hold of herself.

"It's too early to be laughing that hard," he said and turned beet red. He set his coffee onto a coaster on the dining room table and plopped down in the chair.

Irene recovered and started to pile the toast onto the plates. "I didn't think it'd be so easy to make a cop blush. And why did you ask what my size was?"

"I think I've got a few of those what do you call them . . . spaghetti tops in my top drawer? And maybe some shorts, too." He ran his hands over his cheeks. "No lingerie, though, sorry."

"I'd start to question my safety if you did." She brought his plate out to him first, then went back into the kitchen for her own as well as her tea. "Did you ever have to dress up like a woman, you know . . . for one of those . . . dragnets?"

"Would it bother you if I wanted to change the topic?"

Irene picked up her egg and started to tap it against her plate. "Yes. But since I already embarrassed you this morning once, it's only fair to say that you don't have to answer the question," she chuckled again softly.

He shoved a corner of the toast into his mouth and regained some of his composure. "Maybe I will later on." Seconds later, he felt his fingers tremble as his phone rang. "This is Armstrong."

"Good morning to you, too, Tiger," a familiar South African accent pleasantly greeted him.

Why are all the women in my current life so chipper this morning? Am I the only one who got robbed of sleep last night?

"Oh, hello there. Where'd you end up sleeping last night?"

"Your man Falk gave me a cot, and I ended up in his office. Though honestly, his couch was much more comfortable, and I spent the night on that after he left."

"Right. So, what did he find with Franklin? Anything weird?"

"Oh, not much, just these little nanite machines that are attached to nearly every single red and white blood cell in his entire body. And . . . yes . . . after I told Franklin that we'd given him sugar water and not cancer, he strove to asphyxiate me," Liszt remarked sardonically. "I wasn't exactly expecting complete gratitude, but I certainly didn't expect to receive *that* reaction. Naturally, I lived to tell the tale."

That would depend upon how you worded your revelation. I think I've lost count of how many times the thought has crossed my mind to do the same to you.

Armstrong began to also peel off the outside shell. "He did what?"

"He tried to choke me. Was I not clear?"

"Not really, no. I was making sure that I heard your side of the story correctly," he stated. "I'm glad you're okay, though."

"Didn't know you cared, Tiger."

He cleared his throat and salted his egg. "From a professional standpoint, I meant."

"Of course." She paused on the line. "Are you eating breakfast? Did I call you at a bad time?"

"No, go ahead, if you've got more things to say."

"I do, and I can confirm that Falk is not privy to whatever McGregor is doing or hiding from us. He also stipulates that he will not assist McGregor if his motivation is to take the cure for himself because of its nature. Franklin said a few times that he had to obey someone . . . didn't specifically say who or why, other than the fact that we were interfering with something. Sounds like he might have been brainwashed. How was your extraction, by the way? What about Honda; can he be trusted?"

Armstrong shook his head. "I don't know that. Irene is safe right now and is sitting beside me."

"Was it a cozy night?"

He rolled his eyes and shoved some of the egg into his mouth. Armstrong chose to give her a smart aleck reply just to see what her reaction would be. He was one hundred percent sure that she would take the bait. "Jealous that I didn't invite you, too?"

The pause on the line made his ego surge; she hadn't expected him to make a retort like that this time. What she said next made him a tad more uncomfortable. "If there's anything that I've learned so far in life, it's this. A hard man . . . is good to find. And he who hesitates is last."

Armstrong swallowed his bite quickly; that was almost twice now in less than half an hour that another woman practically made him blush. Both of these women only did it with words! *Is today a national holiday for sexual innuendoes or something? If it is, then nobody told me about it.*

He shelved his embarrassment and steered the conversation back onto topic. "Something really odd happened last night. I threatened Honda with my gun, then he brought up a shield to deflect my shots, he snapped his fingers, and then somehow, a fire started in the house!"

"Didn't that Captain McCully say that it was due to poor electrical wiring?" Irene broke in.

"Sure, that's what he said, but I have a feeling that your uncle wouldn't stand for that. Look at how the rest of that house was built, Irene. It's nearly like the Chrysler building!"

"Well, regardless of that, it's now highly likely that we can't trust Honda either," Liszt observed.

"Don't jump to conclusions, Harriet. I saw Honda taking photos of all these false documents with his magnafone, and he said that this new discovery about McGregor was too much for him to handle by himself. He needed a federal agency's help; maybe he went to the NSA or the FBI about McGregor," Armstrong rebuked her civilly. "I appreciate your caution, though. The lines of friend and enemy are becoming pretty blurry to read between these days."

"Then why did you shoot at him?"

"Because he wouldn't stand down when I directly asked him about his loyalties. I gave him several chances to do so, and he dismissed me every single time. He practically called me ungrateful right to my face." Armstrong took another bite of his egg. "I also couldn't take the chance that he'd hurt Irene somehow."

"At least we got out okay," Irene reminded him. "The house didn't totally burn down, either, and we got a lot of those false papers on our way out."

"Did you hear that, Liszt?" Armstrong inquired.

"Yes, I did. That's good, because I have something more to tell you," Liszt replied.

"What's that?"

"If you'll recall two nights ago, I handed a burner over to McGregor after I played back the audio for everyone's benefit."

"Yes, I do."

"As you will come to know me better, Armstrong, you'll learn that I am an extremely cautious person who plans ahead."

I had no idea. Perhaps you should have told me that earlier . . . oh wait; you already did. Several times now.

"An ounce of caution is worth a pound of a cure," Armstrong said.

"Precisely. There is a back up file of those phone calls that is hidden somewhere very safe elsewhere in the city . . . in San Francisco, I mean. And I can get it practically whenever I'd like. However, until we're absolutely positive about Honda's or McGregor's motivations, it will stay there."

"Did you just say 'we'? Yesterday and the day before that, it was only 'I'." He paused to shove the rest of the egg into his mouth. "Just so we know where you and I stand, that is."

There was a long pause on the line before she answered him. "I suppose I did, yes."

"Are you gonna retract your statement, or is this an actual partnership that we're talking about here?"

"Alliances are wise investments, and I'm a very prudent person when it comes to those. I never finance something I'm not absolutely sure of."

Guess that's an oh yeah, Tiger. Read in between the lines; she wants you to think. That's why she's playing hard to get, and that's why sometimes . . . that makes a very good partner. You don't choose them; they choose you.

He licked his lips unconsciously; Irene noticed this but said nothing and took another sip of her tea. "Then let's say that we make an actual arrangement, here. Say that we agree to—son of a bitch!" His fingers tingled him as his phone told him that he had an incoming call. It was from McGregor. Maybe this mystery could all end today.

"What just happened? Are you all right?"

"I'm fine. McGregor's calling me. Don't go anywhere; I'll call you back in an hour, okay?"

"Danger is something I've become quite accustomed to in this line of work, Armstrong. But for you . . . since we've become . . . attached as it were, I promise."

Now Armstrong felt just as perplexed as he had earlier in the conversation when Liszt had told him about the super-nanites. *I don't care what anybody says. The biggest mystery of the universe is still what goes on in a woman's head. I don't think that modern technology could ever make a good enough translator for a man to understand it.*

"This is Armstrong."

"How soon can you get to St. Petersburg, Florida?" McGregor's voice nearly tore through his eardrums, causing him to wince.

"Good morning to you too, sir."

"Did you just wake up?"

"No, I've been awake for about three quarters of an hour now, and I've just finished my breakfast. What can I do for you, Mr. McGregor?" *I guess I am still employed as of this moment.*

"I would ask Honda to meet me here, but I can't get in touch with him. Either he's turned his phone off, or he won't accept my calls."

"There's a reason for that, sir. Both of us found out some very interesting information about you just yesterday. Just who in the hell are you?"

"What are you talking about?" McGregor inquired.

"Your name isn't really McGregor. I don't know what it is, and frankly at this point, I don't give a rat's ass. I'd rather know why you've sent me on this wild goose chase. Do you want this cure for cancer for yourself, or do you just want to expose Sondheim to the world?"

"That's not important right now. What is—"

"The hell it isn't, sir. Excuse my excitement, but I've seen more action in the last two days than James Bond! There have been more twists and turns in this crazy story than an Alfred Hitchcock thriller." He calmed down and lowered the volume of his voice. "Well, maybe it's not that bad, now that I come to think of it . . . no one's tried to take a knife to me in the shower yet."

"There's always a first time," Irene remarked.

"You need to get here . . . *now*. I'm meeting with someone who's got a very incredible story about this cure for cancer. He can clear a lot of this mystery up for us, but I need you physically here to see him," McGregor insisted.

"Why were you in St. Petersburg in the first place, sir? It's not exactly a great time of the year for fishing or lying on the beach."

"I was going to plan a heist to get into Sondheim headquarters to attempt to retrieve this cure. However, before I could do that, I needed Honda's help, and like I said before, he's not answering my phone calls, text messages, or emails."

Armstrong sighed. *I really hate to repeat myself so much, but it looks like I'm going to have to do it again.*

"Why do you want this cure, sir? Is it for the profit? The power? Do you know what the side effects are to this cure?"

There was silence on the other end of the line as McGregor thought through his response. Armstrong chose to reveal one more piece of information to him.

"Irene is with me, and I won't go anywhere without her, sir."

"You can confirm her safety, then," McGregor finally spoke. "If you're trying to extort me . . ."

"I'm hoping to avoid it, but yes, she is safe."

"Go to my office. Inside my safe is a spare townhouse key. The access code for this week should be coming to your magnafone in a text message in about two minutes. If Irene doesn't want to come with you or if you feel that it's too dangerous, give it to her; she'll be safe there. Bring Liszt with you. This story is far too incredible for just your ears alone. I'm sure that she's also been rather interested to learn more about this ordeal."

That's putting it mildly. She'd probably shoot you in the knee first and ask questions later.

"Do I have to make a decision now? Can't I come there tomorrow?" Armstrong wondered.

"I will tell you what you need to know after you get here. No, you cannot come tomorrow. Hermes will be leaving Earth is in less than a day's time. I don't know if he'll ever return to our planet or even have the means to fix the horrible mess that Sondheim has gotten our species into."

Armstrong put down his coffee onto his table. "I'm sorry, sir, I'm just not much of a morning person. Or maybe I'm starting to hear things. Did you just say what I thought you just said?"

"Yes. My acquaintance here . . . is not of this world. And neither is the one who gave the cure to Sondheim."

That's it; I think I've gone off the deep end. I am officially nuts.

"I understand that your brain has probably gone into overload," McGregor continued. "I was quite shocked to hear it myself."

More like a meltdown, actually.

"But if you don't get here today, we, the human race, are officially doomed." Without waiting for a response, McGregor disconnected the call.

Armstrong covered his face with his hands and leaned his elbows onto the table.

"What did my uncle, um, McGregor, whoever he is now . . . what did he say?" Irene pressed him.

"Something that will likely split your mind in two," he replied through the palms of his hands.

"Was it good or bad? I can't exactly tell by your body language, and I'm usually pretty good at reading that from people."

"Bad, if I don't go to Florida today."

"Florida?!" Her face was incredulous, and then she lifted a finger to her lips as she thought. "Oh, I get it. Sondheim's headquarters are there. Well, are you going to go there or not?"

He pressed his fingers to his forehead and leaned back in his chair. "Your uncle . . . let's still call him that for now . . . just told me something that totally changes life as we humans know it."

"How so?"

"That's why I have to go to Florida."

Irene stood up, collected their plates, and went into the kitchen with them. "Well, what's stopping you from doing that?" she asked.

"What about you? I have no clue what on earth I'm going to be stepping into when I get down there, and I can't leave you here unprotected!"

"If I remember correctly, didn't you have some kind of phone call to make to your partner?" She started to rinse the dishes off.

Partner? We never actually agreed to-

"Hello? Nestor? Are you on Earth, or did you go to another planet?" Irene came back into the dining room and passed a hand over his face.

"That might actually happen," he mumbled to himself.

"What?"

"Nothing. Yeah, I've gotta call Liszt. Thanks for reminding me, Irene."

"No prob. I'm gonna go take a shower. Oh, wait a minute, before I do that. Where did you say that those women's clothes were?"

"Top drawer in my chest."

"You know, it's a little scary how fast you just knew that off the top of your head like that. You still owe me an explanation for why those clothes are there in the first place, by the way."

She whizzed by him and hurried into his bedroom. With a loud sigh, Armstrong shuffled back into the kitchen and refilled his mug. He glanced at the coffee maker's clock. *It's not even eight o'clock in the morning, and my brain feels like it's been going non-stop for the past forty-eight hours. Oh well. Time to give Dirty Harriet a buzz.*

"I was wondering if I'd hear from you soon," her silky voice brushed against his eardrums. It was about ten times more pleasant than McGregor's raspy tone.

"Have I got you on pins and needles?" he kept his tone playful.

"What did McGregor say?"

"A lot. In fact, I believe the world is still spinning . . . is there any chance you could make it stop, please?"

"I might need a bit more information than that to do so."

"He seemed genuinely concerned about his niece Irene, and he just sent a text to me with an access code to the safe in his office. He wants me to take her there or bring her with me."

"Bring her with you? Where are you going, all of a sudden?"

Armstrong recounted McGregor's story to her, which took about five minutes' time. She remained totally reticent until his last comment, and then she offered her opinion after he asked. "I can watch over Irene while you go to St. Petersburg if you'd like. The closest major airport to it is Tampa, right?"

"Yes, but I might be able to get a flight into Albert Whitted. It's smaller but more convenient. Their business has grown up a bit more over the years, as I understand it."

"What're you scheming?"

"I'm sending you my address. Meet me here in person, and let's talk about it. I'm not crazy about phone conversations."

"All right. I'll be over in about forty-five minutes or so. Have you got your coffee brewing?"

"I can always make some more. Why? Didn't you get any in the break room this morning?"

"Unfortunately not, and by the way, that reminds me to tell you something. Your coffee on demand machine might need to be replaced."

He closed his eyes and internally counted to ten. "What happened?" *I hope she didn't shoot it.*

"I haven't the damnedest idea. One of Falk's employees had it torn apart in pieces on the counter when I got there. And there was no more espresso; needless to say, I still need a bit of a jump start this morning."

"It'll be ready for you by the time you get here."

"That's kind of you. See you soon, Tiger." She hung up, and Armstrong took a glance around his apartment.

Unlike most bachelors, he kept everything fairly neat and in order. No dishes were left on the counters with food rotting on them, the trash never piled up, and he kept his bathroom spotless. The only thing that he let go was the coffee table. Sometimes, that would become cluttered with stacks of paper or whatever back copies of law enforcement magazines he had been perusing.

He wished that he had a fireplace. That was the only thing that was missing to make his love life better, or so one girl had told him. Strangely enough, he couldn't remember if she was named Laura or Lauren. "What does it matter . . . I always go for the same type anyhow," he mused to himself. "Looks like I might be doing it again." His gaze went to the bathroom; he was tempted to open the door and take a peak but decided against it. She was vulnerable right now. Like a good white knight, here he came to sweep her off of her feet and save her from the evil duke that might still be her uncle.

Maybe McGregor wasn't evil, and maybe neither was Honda.

He stretched his arms up to the ceiling and wiggled his fingertips. "Today would be a good day to go to the range and get some of these damned questions off of my mind," he told himself aloud. "Too bad I can't go."

Well, there's only one way I can deal with this for now.

After he started the coffee maker again to make a fresh pot of coffee, Armstrong picked up the acoustic guitar next to his flat panel TV, and started to strum along with a simple string track to the Beatles' song "Yesterday". In a mildly pleasant tenor voice, he began to sing along with it. He forgot half of the words to the second verse and hummed along instead.

The door to his bathroom opened, and Irene quietly tiptoed out with a towel wrapped around her chest to hear him. The whole scene made her smile, but she quickly ran back into the bedroom just before the song came to a close.

CHAPTER NINE

Armstrong's Apartment, San Francisco, CA July 18th, 2079, 0817h

While he waited for Liszt to arrive, Armstrong had called Falk to give him an update on how matters had changed from in Falk's words "pretty interesting" to "pretty damned confusing". Falk offered to go pick up the key from McGregor's safe in the meanwhile and refused to accept the access code text that Armstrong tried to send him. He told Armstrong that his brain needed the extra stimulation today; he'd rather crack it open. Besides, it would give him a new record time to beat.

When Armstrong asked Falk how many times he had broken into McGregor's office safe, Falk refused to answer. Instead, he answered another question that Armstrong had asked him in the past. He finally told Nestor where he had been born and raised, which was Belfast.

A knock came to his door; not only did Liszt come but so did Falk. They stood just beside one another as Armstrong answered it. "I hope you two didn't carpool," he smirked.

Falk's eyes went over to Liszt, who merely rolled hers. "It's a long story," she replied to his unasked question.

"No, we didn't," the Irishman told Armstrong. "I'm here to collect Miss McGregor."

"But, I thought that . . . well . . .—"

"Are you going to invite us in, or are we going to stand on your bloody doorstep like a couple of Jehovah's Witnesses?" Falk's hands went to his hips.

"Sorry." Armstrong opened the door all the way, they filed inside, and he shut it quietly behind them. "Nathan, I thought that you were going to break into McGregor's safe and get the key."

"Your apartment is on the way to the office, and Ms. Liszt mentioned that his niece needed some protection."

"Nestor, what's . . . going . . . on?" Irene inquired as she came out, thankfully fully clothed. "Oh, hi. Irene McGregor . . . well, actually . . . it's just Irene for now, I guess." She reached for Nathan's hand, and he took it. Instead of shaking it, he brought it up to his lips.

"A pleasure, Miss McGregor. Nathan Falk."

"Oh, that reminds me," Armstrong said and snapped his fingers. He disappeared into his bedroom, brought the badly burned 'Spidey' polymer nano-suit back out, and bravely put it into Falk's hands.

The Irishman growled angrily and raised his fist at Armstrong. "I swear, boy, if these two ladies weren't present, you'd feel not only this, but the wrath of Jack Dempsey, too."

"Jack who?" Armstrong's eyebrows knit together.

"A boxer from the twentieth century of Irish descent. Never you mind. Are you ready to go, Miss McGregor?"

"I'll be right back, Mr. Falk." Irene journeyed back down the hallway while Armstrong fetched a mug from his cupboards and poured some coffee for Liszt. They nearly arrived back at the same time, but Armstrong beat Irene just by a hair.

"Lucky for you, that other 'Spidey' suit has just been fixed for your sojourn down to the hubs of Hell. Stop by the armory before you go out of town, lad. It'll be waiting for ya there," Falk instructed him.

"Thank you, Nathan."

Irene warily glanced at the Irishman, then at Armstrong, who gave her a nod as if to say 'I trust him; you'll be okay'.

"When will I see you again?" she demanded.

Armstrong shook his head. "I don't know, honestly. But Falk will take care of you; he's a good friend of mine."

"Well, just in case I don't ever get to say this to you again, I wanted to thank you for all that you've done for me. I'm not sure that Honda would have intentionally hurt me, but . . . you're a really brave guy, and I can appreciate that." She leaned forward to kiss his cheek and even closer towards his ear. "You've got a really sexy singing voice, by the way," she cooed.

Armstrong felt himself grow a little hotter at her sudden and unexpected proximity. He gave her a smile in return, partially because he was embarrassed, and he squeezed her shoulder. "Take care of yourself, Irene."

The two of them left the apartment, and he padded back into the kitchen to attend to his own beverage. Liszt situated herself on the couch beside his guitar and mewled happily into her coffee after consuming about a quarter of it. "Tops coffee, Armstrong, such a lovely blend. I'm quite partial to either Colombian or Puerto Rican, but I'm not one to complain if this is neither," she commented.

"It's Kona coffee, actually, from Hawaii," Armstrong informed her. "I'd love to go there one day, but, well . . .—"

"So, what was it that you wanted to discuss?" Her eyes spotted what appeared to be a pile of drink coasters on a completely filled bookshelf; she took two from it and put them onto the table in front of them both. She then set her mug onto the one in front of her.

"You. Us. Our work."

"Right, well, I've given it some thought, and to tell you the truth, I had a rather difficult time last night getting very much sleep. I also wanted to apologize for my rude behavior earlier . . . when I stomped on your foot yesterday, I mean." She glanced downward at her lavender blouse and removed a piece of fuzz from it.

That's strangely comforting, he thought. *Wait a second here. She's apologizing?* "Yeah, me, too—I meant about sleeping."

"I normally don't give rocks about having a partner, but . . . it's unusual for me to admit when I need help."

"I think we're more alike than you give me credit." He crossed one leg on top of the other. "There's something about me that you should know, though."

Liszt turned her body towards him, leaned her hand on her chin, and set her elbow onto the back of the couch with complete interest.

"Back when I was a homicide detective, I had a partner. It's rare for that to happen nowadays, and well, Lisa was . . . more than that to me."

"You were close?"

He licked his lips unconsciously. "Yeah . . . so much so that . . . that my captain almost separated the two of us from working with one another."

"Why didn't he? Did you two break it off?"

"No. Lisa got shot while we were trying to negotiate with a suspect and a hostage. It was right in the stomach," his voice cracked while he recounted this and placed his hand over his own. "I overreacted and killed the son of a bitch instead of arresting him. Then I called for an ambulance, for her, I mean."

"Did she . . .—"

"Yeah, well, I mean, no, she didn't make it. I held her in my arms for I don't know how long . . . didn't even bother to ask the hostage if he was okay or anything. All I cared about was her." His eyes met hers; her expression had been stoic until the present. Now her visage held an expression of sympathy. "I got heavily reprimanded for my actions as the case was reviewed and suspended from duty in order to recuperate or what have you, but . . . I only returned back to the force for another six months. Then I left; I couldn't take it anymore. I could never bring myself to clean out her desk or her locker. And those clothes that you saw Irene wearing belonged to Lisa."

"What was she like? Or do you not feel comfortable talking about that?"

He was surprised that she asked him that question. He didn't think that she'd be the type of person to be sensitive to matters like this; however, he did go on. "She was outgoing and very sweet. She loved to laugh at my innuendos and return her own. Sometimes she'd come up with ones that made me even blush. And she could sew."

"Really?"

"I have a handkerchief with my initials on it that she embroidered. It's probably lying in a drawer in my night stand somewhere. I haven't carried it since . . . well ever since . . .—"

"I'm sorry to hear that. We've all got our own . . . baggage as it were." She glanced down at the locket that rested on her heart and opened it. Moments later, she undid the clasp from the back of her neck, and gave the necklace to him so he could look at her father's picture. "I told you that he died when I was fifteen, just after my birthday."

"His name was Meredith, right? I think I remember that, too."

She nodded sullenly. "I absolutely had to see the Kuai Twang in concert, so a limousine dropped me off. I remember getting a text from my dad telling me that he had called off the driver, and that he was coming to pick me up on his motorcycle that night. It felt so good that he . . . he wanted to make sure that I was safe. I don't know if you've ever heard about the history that's been a part of my country for the last several hundred years, but apartheid *still* remains in South Africa, probably to this very day. It's not safe for a teenage girl to be roaming about anywhere late at night, but it's especially bad in Cape Town."

Shit. That's why she-

"We rode back. It was just after one a.m., and he lost control over the bike when he accidentally slid over some oil in the road. Seconds later, the cycle spun into a tree. I fortunately was wearing a helmet but he wasn't." She took a drink from her mug again. "He died instantly."

"You said something about you and your step-mother having a disagreement. Was that about what happened to your dad?"

Liszt nodded. "Mmm . . . she blamed me for his death. She said that if I hadn't demanded to go to the concert, then he'd still be alive. I can't help but wonder—"

"That's ridiculous. If he had gotten hit by a bus while walking across the street, could either of you have done something about it?"

He surprised himself by how passionate he became and noticed that he had even started to clutch the locket. Armstrong relaxed himself, looked down at the picture again, and then up at Liszt. "You have his eyes. I wish I knew what my parents looked like," he remarked and gave the locket back to her finally.

"You said that you were raised by Native Americans. Do you know what happened to your parents?" she gently inquired.

"No. No one could tell me anything about them because I'd been found in a dumpster just outside of a restaurant as an infant."

Her jaw flew open with disbelief. "That's disgusting. People who do that should be lined up against a wall and shot." She closed it and crossed her arms against her chest. "I'd have no problem handling those sorts of executions."

"And what about the ones that I saw you commit?"

Liszt's eyes snapped over towards his. "I had no choice. They were opening fire on us, remember? Live rounds?"

"But I had a non-lethal weapon; I could have just knocked them down with my luke," he argued. "Did you actually like working at Sondheim?"

"Yes, I found it rather challenging and intriguing. There was always some chop who was trying to break down our company's firewalls or finagle his way into one of our scientist's minds to attempt to get the magical formula. The people there were good, for the most part. Wooster was very good with delegation; he told me to do whatever I needed to do to make our company safe. It wasn't until I ran across that phone call that I even gave one thought about betraying Sondheim."

"So that's it, then, huh? The end justifies the means? If our roles had been reversed while we were escaping Bethesda, would you have killed those guards, too?"

"No, of course not. They weren't using bullets," she shook her head. "I would have used Leontine to defend myself . . . . us, I mean. Falk went through a lot of trouble to make that gun for me, and I very much look forward to a time when I can actually make some use of it." She shook her head 'no', and he arose to take his guitar back towards the TV to lean it up against the wall. "I wish I could still remember how to play the clarinet. My father hired one when I was in grammar school. I quit after he passed on."

"Ever think about taking lessons again?"

She leaned forward and took another drink of coffee. "Maybe. My step-mother refused to pay for them afterward. I left home a year later because I couldn't take her constant belittling anymore. Every time I came home with a card that had less than excellent marks on it, she grounded me for a week."

"That's pretty harsh." Armstrong's eyebrows furrowed. "She punished you because you didn't get all "A"s?"

"And she made me sleep in the servants' quarters. It wasn't horrible, but there was no air conditioning inside those. The mosquitoes and gnats were absolutely dreadful just before dusk and just after dawn. They always managed to creep inside those nets somehow; thankfully Dad had me inoculated much earlier in life. I had shared a bedroom with one of her two daughters previously, but then after Dad died, she kicked me out."

"You didn't have to put on an apron and start to serve everyone, did you?"

"No, but I'm sure that that might have been the next step had I not left the premises." She bit her lip and guzzled down some more java. "She was a horrible woman to begin with . . . I don't see how my father was ever attracted to her."

He sighed and shook his head. "So, about us . . . where are we?"

Her eyes met his again. "I'd like to keep working together. Falk's proven himself trustworthy, and you . . . well . . . you've managed to put up with me so far."

"You know, there have been some times that . . . it's been . . . difficult. What're you trying to prove? I'm not your enemy here." Armstrong came closer to the couch towards her; he was now about three feet away.

"I know that now." A smirk crept across her face. "I was expecting the word bitch to make it into one of those sentences, actually."

"Although it's never come out of my mouth, my mind has certainly used it a lot," he chuckled. "I . . . it's been three years for me since I started work with Zionastra. And it's been four since I lost Lisa. With all that's been going on here, I . . ."

"Both of us need each other for now." Her expression became serious, and she stood up from the couch. In a much more submissive voice, she went on. "I think it'd be to our advantage to cooperate, don't you think?" She laid a hand onto his abdomen.

He glanced downward at her hand and felt his pulse quicken. It was indeed a bold move on her behalf but not an unwelcome one.

"Do you trust me, Nestor?"

Armstrong licked his lips unconsciously and again made eye contact with her when she called him by his first name. *She's never done that before. What's going on here?*

"I . . . I think I do," he replied nervously.

"I need to know so that we can plan our next move. I'm not asking how you feel about McGregor or Honda or even Irene at this point. I don't give rocks at the moment, actually, about the three of them. I want to know how you feel about us."

His head was swimming now; he wasn't sure if it was the caffeine that was doing it, the lack of sleep, or perhaps some adrenaline. *I went through all those women trying to make them measure up to Lisa. Even Irene is almost a carbon copy of sorts. There's something different about Penelope. Maybe I need to stop trying to keep making the same type of cookies and . . . goddamn it all . . .*

Armstrong decided to take a very large gambit. He leaned forward, seized her by the waist, and planted his lips onto her. A part of his ego leapt into the air when she didn't fight him or pull away; she merely accepted his actions. In fact, he became a tad more bold and deepened their kiss into an open-mouthed one. He gently pulled upon her lips with his, and that same hand that had been on his abdomen grabbed a fistful of his t-shirt.

The other hand reached up towards his jaw and cupped it as she hungrily returned his passion. But then, just when he was about to increase his fervor, she released his t-shirt and pulled away from him. They both were breathing incredibly hard at this point. She stepped backward and was reminded that the sofa was just behind her. Thankfully, she had some presence of mind to keep her balance, but it was not by much. "Shit, what . . . what just happened?" she muttered.

"I . . . I'm sorry, I . . ." For once, he was completely speechless. Words seemed to be failing him more now than ever. He tried to gauge her body language. She wasn't angry; she was flustered and also seemed to have the same problem now as he.

Finally, about five seconds later, she found her voice. "We . . . we've been through a lot. The last two days have been so . . .—"

"Stressful?"

"Oweh, they have," Liszt replied. "I . . . what were we talking about?"

"Us. And I uh . . . unfortunately uh . . . may have overstepped my bounds here."

"No. Well . . . we both did," she admitted and began to regain her composure. "Look, it's best that we forget that this happened . . . for now and just . . . try to focus on business."

"Yeah," he agreed and bit his lip. *It was a mistake, that's all.*

"Do you want me to stay behind and protect Irene here, or do you trust Falk to do it? I just want to be sure here." Liszt made eye contact with him and took another few steps backward from him.

"No, I trust him, and I trust you, too. Let's go to Florida."

The professional mask that she wore slid right back onto her face naturally. "I'll book us some transportation while you go arm yourself."

"Sounds good." He traveled back into his bedroom, put on some socks and shoes, then came back out with his magnafone.

"By the way, that Spidey suit isn't fireproof?"

"No, it isn't. Maybe Falk will make that improvement. I'll take the Muni to the police station. I had a friend impound my bike for me."

"Do you mind if I stay here for a while to do my web browsing?"

"Not at all. Make yourself at home." Armstrong pocketed his magnafone and made his way towards the door; he noticed that she was watching him with a piqued curiosity.

And wipe that damned smirk off of your face, she thought. *I know that it's there . . . arrogant rascal.*

McGregor Townhouse, San Francisco, CA
July 18th, 2079, 1019h

Irene found herself dragging her feet more than usual this morning, and it wasn't because of the tranquilizers that Armstrong had given to her from the previous night. Being thrown into a major corporate conspiracy was certainly not an everyday experience to her, nor was it to follow quirky but brilliant Irish American scientists around. If she had been able to make that audition last night, in about half an hour, she would have been doing chassées across a studio floor. That was just not the card that the deck of fate had played for her.

However, after Falk had broken into McGregor's safe, he assured her that she could completely trust him. Even now, as he slid the key card across the street door's sensor, she still felt nervous. The LED went from amber to green, and the door automatically opened. A synthesized female voice gave the both of them a cheery greeting, and a coat rack slid towards them on a rail. "Oh, that's pretty ingenious if I do say so myself," Falk stated with a bemused chortle. "I almost wish that it were raining so I could hang up a poncho on it."

"It's creepy," Irene commented and shrank away from it. "If the lights didn't pop on when we entered, too, I probably would have screamed."

"Are you still frightened, child? Don't be." Falk pointed to himself. "I won the flyweight title in an amateur boxing competition back home. Marquess of Queensberry rules, you know."

"I'm still not sure about my uncle or . . . whoever he is," she said with an uneasy shrug. "Or about Mr. Honda."

"Well, Honda knows about this place but wouldn't dare to come here, especially if he is trying to find out the truth about McGregor. He's got bigger fish to fry, so to speak." He placed a hand onto his hip, and the other stroked his chin as he thought. "He's got his own evidence, from what Armstrong told me. And it's likely that he'll try to pursue that and nothing else."

"So you've known Mr. Honda for a long time, then. It was so odd that he could start a fire like that with nothing but the snap of his fingers." She walked into the kitchen, and the lights turned themselves on as Falk pursued her.

"Ah, yes, well, I wouldn't say that the fire came completely out of nowhere. In order to keep a fire going, you need three things: heat, energy, and fuel. If you remove one of those, then you can smother the fire. And Honda had some help."

"How's that?" She opened the refrigerator door and removed a container of strawberries from the fruit drawer. Irene started to open the kitchen's drawers to look for a knife.

"Can I help you find something?" The synthesized deep female voice asked that greeted them when they came inside the house frightened both of its occupants.

"Oh, shit!" Irene exclaimed and whirled about, accidentally slamming herself into a counter behind. Falk's eyes and head merely tried to locate the source of their mysterious visitor. "Um . . . who are you?"

"So he *did* end up using her. Damn that cheap bastard," Falk growled and banged his fist onto a counter nearby. "This is Ilsa, short for *I*ntel *L*igent *S*ynthetic *A*ssistant. One of my associates made her six years ago. Ilsa was supposed to be some sort of artificial intelligence program that could interface with the implant at the back of your neck to check the internet for whatever medical questions you had or could tell you which type of doctor you needed to report to when you said that you weren't feeling well. She can also monitor vital signs and make suggestions to help you live longer."

"That is my secondary objective in my programming, Mr. Falk. The first is to serve humans however I can. The third is to do—"

"I know Asimov's three rules, Ilsa," Falk said and rolled his eyes. "Do you have a platform, or are you wired directly into a server here in the house somewhere?"

"After you stepped inside the door, you began to walk through my body. I am Mr. McGregor's house," the synthetic voice replied neutrally.

"Fine, whatever," Irene sighed impatiently. "Do you know where the pear knives are?"

Three seconds later, a drawer to her left immediately opened. "Thanks, Ilsa, was it? And why do you say that my uncle's a cheap bastard?"

"Because he dismissed the idea right off the bat and wouldn't give my assistant the time of the day with it. He must have gotten Honda to get a copy of it later on after everyone went home for the day," Falk realized. "Anyway, back to the original explanation I was going to give you here. Honda didn't start that fire all by himself. There was also some technology that I was working on years ago. It's something that can help a person focus all of his or her energy on in their mind and make it happen."

Irene started to run the strawberries under the sink's sensor to clean them, and water immediately poured freely out of it. "Uh-huh."

"Honda was a willing participant in this experiment; as a result of this, he has to constantly consume caffeine or calories because his brain is working overtime. This technology also involves nanites that will attach themselves directly to the medulla oblongata and the spinal cord."

"Um . . . Ilsa, are there any bowls around here?" A cupboard to her left opened. "Thanks." She bent down to retrieve one and filled the strawberries with it. "Sorry, you were saying?"

"The direct current that runs through the body gives these nanites power, and they interact with the cerebrum directly," Falk continued.

"But how could Honda just think that he wanted to start a fire?"

"Everywhere on Earth, there is some sort of energy in a room or in nature." He made a gesture to the water faucet as she removed her hands from it, and the flow immediately stopped. "It's a lot easier to focus that energy in a room because it's an enclosed area. If your mind is attuned to it using these nanites, then you can "will" some wiring to go dodgy, make a burning cigarette go out of control, or cause an open flame that's already present to transfer its energy elsewhere. You don't have to necessarily see the energy fields to interact with them; when they're projected, they're not visible to the naked eye since they operate on a different wavelength—on the nano scale, actually."

"Ah, okay." She picked up the pear knife and began to cut the tops of the strawberries off. "But don't most electrical devices have breakers nowadays to prevent that kind of stuff from happening? And nobody was smoking in the room."

"Aye, very astute of you to you know that, Miss McGregor. But most circuits that have ground fault interrupts can be overridden or bypassed by a sensor on the back. Was there a time when you left Honda alone in the room before Armstrong got there?"

"Hmm . . . I did go to the bathroom once."

"Then Honda could have tampered with the GFI. The only person that knew about this experiment was Honda; not even McGregor knows what he can do. This actually all happened by accident. Honda had one day wandered into the lab after everyone had left for day, except me of course, and he wanted to know what I was doing. Since I was not really on the clock anymore but still using Mr. McGregor's equipment . . ."

"You told him, then."

"Yes, to keep him silent, I agreed to let him test it out exclusively. Honda's had this technology for the past three years."

"And what exactly does this tech do?"

"Well, to put it simply, I found a way to interact quarks with wavelength dispersive x-ray spectroscopy through crystals of course and magnons."

"Um . . ."

"Those have to do with the excitations of electron rotations. Anyway, as you know, quarks have six different classifications: up, down, strange, bottom, top, and charm. They actually—"

She held up a hand to stop him and made a sweeping gesture with it over her head. "Sorry, Mr. Falk, that just did this."

"Ah, well . . . I forgot. Particle quantum physics isn't everyone's cup of tea," he chuckled to himself and scratched at some dry skin on the back of his neck. "But Nestor might want to know about this, though; I should probably tell him about it."

Irene set the bowl down in front of the two of them onto the counter and plucked one of the berries out. "How long have you known Nestor?" she inquired.

Falk eyed the strawberries curiously then finally caved to his carnal desires and also took one for himself. "Let's see here, it's been about three years, I think. When he first came into my territory, my lab, that is and heard my accent, the smug jackass made a wisecrack about some leprechaun and asked me if I had any Lucky Charms."

"Isn't that some kind of cereal?"

The Irishman rolled his eyes. "Aye, it is, one meant for kids. I gave him a lesson in respect that day, for both my country's sake and my age." He popped the strawberry into his mouth and chewed thoughtfully. "But understand, missy, that Armstrong is extremely reliable. From day one after that smart aleck response, I knew that I'd grow to like him."

"Yeah?"

"Hmm . . . he'd die before he would let anything happen to you, that I'm sure of. And though I don't know you yet, I do know him and trust him completely. So, any friend of his is a friend of mine, and I'll do my best to protect you."

"And what do you think about my uncle?"

"I'm not sure what to make of all of this myself. There's got to be a good reason why McGregor kept everyone in the dark about his past. Don't get wrong, it's been goddamned frustrating to work for him over the last seventeen years."

"How so?"

"Well, he has high expectations, is sometimes too cheap, and you already know about that incident with Ilsa."

"You should not hold a grudge against Mr. McGregor," the synthesized voice interrupted him.

"Blast it, I don't need a bloody robot telling me what I should be thinking!" He banged his fist against the counter and caused the bowl of strawberries to lightly bounce up and down.

"Please contain your anger, Mr. Falk. Your blood pressure is spiking."

Falk slapped his hands over his face. "How do I shut this damn thing off?"

"I did not realize that I was causing you to become upset, Mr. Falk. I will go into standby mode but continue to monitor your vital signs, if you'd like."

"Unless I start to have a stroke or a damned heart attack, Ilsa, shut the bloody hell up!"

"As you wish, sir."

"Now, where was I, Miss McGregor?"

"It's Irene, Mr. Falk, and you were talking about my uncle's character." She tossed another strawberry into her mouth and gave one to him.

"Aye, I was indeed, thank you. McGregor told Armstrong not to kill anyone at Sondheim, and the weapons I was ordered to give him were all non-lethal. Perhaps that's because McGregor didn't want to draw the attention of the police to our company of course, you know, because of all the rivalry that's been going on in between the two of us."

"Okay, that makes sense," Irene agreed.

"Now let me ask *you* something, Irene."

"Me?"

"Yes. Do you like Nestor? I noticed some chemistry that was starting to heat up there in between the two of you, back in his apartment."

"I admire him a lot, and well . . . yeah, I noticed that, too." A closed mouth smile went across her lips, and she shoved another strawberry into her mouth. "I guess he's not much on PDA, though."

"Well, as much as I'd like to encourage the two of you, it wouldn't be wise to pursue a relationship right now," Falk shook his head.

"Yeah, I have a feeling that I know how it could blow up in my face. I dated a lighting engineer once for about a year. Our relationship went from great to bad in three days, and he'd never fix the overhead lighting specials that were supposed to hit me. In fact, he moved them sometimes in between rehearsal and the show to leave me in the dark on purpose. Sometimes I'd miss my spike, but I'd say about eighty-five percent of the time, I got it. How freaking unprofessional is that? I mean . . . *really*!"

"Remember how you said that my quantum particle physics were going over your head? Well, congratulations, Miss McGregor, you've done the same thing to me," he marveled.

"That's a first; I've never been able to baffle a scientist before," she laughed. "But at least David didn't do anything else to hurt me."

"I'd better see if I can contact my team to check on their progress. If you need me, I'll be making some phone calls in the living room." He ate one last strawberry and made his exit.

CHAPTER TEN

Tierra Verde Marina, St. Petersburg, FL
July 18th, 2079, 2148h

To avoid suspicion, both Armstrong and Liszt wore everyday civilian clothes that would be very common for this time of the year in Florida. He wore a pearl white polo shirt and a beige pair of khaki shorts; she chose to wear a dark lavender spaghetti top and a pair of cream Capris. They rented a car locally and left their baggage inside it while the car remained parked in the marina lot. Just in case there was trouble, he brought along a tiny .40 semi-automatic pistol and wore it round his foot on his ankle. Thankfully, on their trip, he had remembered to bring his licensed concealed weapon permit. The TSA agent who examined his guns waved him through with little to no trouble at all.

Neither he nor Liszt spoke about their kiss throughout the flight. In a way, he was entirely relieved, because she would have been just one more complication to this scenario that he did not really need right now. But he did think about how her lips felt on his more than once during that long flight. He also remembered that she was wearing a very enticing perfume at the time.

By now of course, the scent had worn off, and she did not bother to reapply the perfume because she did not want to attract any mosquitoes or no-seeums.

"Armstrong, are you listening to me?" she inquired and turned her head towards him. They had just left the rental and began to make their way towards McGregor's yacht, which was tied up in the marina.

"Sorry, I didn't understand your question," he replied. "Could you repeat it again, please?"

"I asked you if you've got a contingency plan for this should it go to hell."

"I have to admit that I actually just was going to wing it and start to shoot in that case. Why, did you have something in mind?"

She adjusted her arm holster and made a cursory glance at Leontine. "No. If you draw your gun, I'll do the same and fire without hesitation. Is there a reason why you didn't want to bring that tranquilizer gun with you?"

"I have no clue what's gonna happen here. I'm not gonna take any chances with my . . . um, with our lives, I mean." He lifted his magnafone up to his eyes to stare at the map that McGregor had sent him. "McGregor's boat should be in the next berth from here; it's named the Archangel."

"Your boss has certainly got a knack for Jewish mythos. First "Zion" and now "Archangel"," she mused.

They rounded the corner to a very luxurious yacht that was no shorter than thirty-five feet in length. There were three visible decks; an observation, navigation, and one below that likely had eating and sleeping quarters. "Damn, this is the life. I can only guess what kind of a boat Sondheim owns," Armstrong remarked.

"Actually, he owns his own train in South Carolina as well as a house there. However, I hear that the property used to belong to his parents. Wooster used to own his own yacht, too, but then he sold it. He said that owning and maintaining a boat can lead to a very large hole in your bank account, which I do not doubt at all."

McGregor's head popped out from the quarters below the navigation deck. "It's about time you two got here. Hermes is down below with me," he announced and made a gesture with his hand to beckon them onto the boat.

Seconds later, a minute gangway that was about three feet long extended itself towards the dock. After Armstrong and Liszt crossed it; the gangway retreated, and they walked down a short set of stairs to meet up with their party. McGregor poured himself a brandy from a rectangular jar full of the beverage, and his visitor sat on a chair with its back to the portholes.

Hermes appeared to look just like any other human; a full glass of sweating water sat in front of him on a table upon a coaster undisturbed. He had jade eyes, dark brown hair, and was clean shaven. His outward appearance was definitely appealing, and Hermes wore a dark navy blue polo shirt as well as a pair of beige colored pants.

"The two of you are humans Armstrong and Liszt?" he addressed them but did not get up. "I am known as Hermes."

"Yes, we are." Armstrong approached him first and held out his hand. Hermes stared briefly at it, then his eyes, and returned the polite gesture. "I'm Armstrong."

"Excuse my skepticism, please, but you don't look all that different from any other kind of human being," Liszt stated coldly. She did not shake his hand and kept her distance.

"This is an illusion, and the voice that you hear is being modulated. I have disguised myself so that you would not be alarmed when you first saw me," Hermes calmly replied. "Would you care to see me in my true form?"

"Have you seen him?" Armstrong asked McGregor, who nodded.

"Would you care for a drink first?"

"No, I'm all right. I think I'd like to see you for real, Hermes. Any objections, Liszt?"

"None at all," she answered him noncommittally and crossed her arms.

"As you wish," Hermes said and touched his bare arm. Less than a second later, the alien transmogrified into a ghastly terrifying spider-like creature. His head was an upside down isosceles triangular shape, and the coloring of it was reminiscent of a red back spider. Hermes had two rows of amber eyes with no pupils; the first row was exactly where a human's would be, and the second pair fell at forty-five degree angles just beneath the first.

He had four arms in total; two of them were currently retracted underneath the first pair, and he had two legs much like a human. He likely had an exoskeleton like his distant relatives here on Earth, and his mouth had two fangs that extruded themselves from it as well as a full set of canine teeth. He did still wear clothes, though these looked to actually be some sort of armor. The armor perfectly matched the color of his head and his skin's noir pigmentation.

Armstrong leapt into the air and hit his head onto the low ceiling with a slight bump. "Ow! Damn, you weren't kidding."

Liszt's eyebrows arose, and even she took a step backward from Hermes' terrifying mien. "Well, that makes sense."

"How can you speak our language?"

"I have a built in translator; it is included in the same program that I use to modify my voice," Hermes responded. His voice was rough and unpleasant; it sounded as if a whole swarm of bees were talking. "My time is limited here on your planet."

"Yes, McGregor mentioned the fact that you had to leave Earth tomorrow. Is this still true?" Armstrong demanded.

"I was to return to my system as soon as possible; my timeline is short. I was to report to my superiors tomorrow when I made contact with you, and since I have done that, I will make contact with them in due time," Hermes told them.

"Just where do you come from?" Liszt wondered. "What is your species called?"

"I realize that this is a great deal for your relatively small minds to comprehend, and I do not mean to insult you by stating that." He placed a claw-like hand over his chest; he had four talons. "I represent the Ochrana; my mission is to use whatever means are necessary to keep the peace in between our people and the Feindliche."

"The who?" Armstrong interrupted him and sat down onto a barstool.

"It would be best if I started to share this with you from the beginning of what I know, then. Two years ago, a fellow human male being upon your planet was visited from the enemy of my people, who are named the Feindliche. He gave Quinn Sondheim the means to cure to a major disease that has for so long plagued your planet. As you might have discovered, this cure unfortunately has a trap built into it. When these nanites are consumed through your blood stream, they start to cause a subtle change in behavior, eventually turning the specimen into a willingly devoted obedient subject," Hermes went on.

"That explains the president of Bethesda's odd reactions," Liszt said with a nod.

"What happened?" McGregor broke in.

"He tried to kill me and kept saying 'I must obey' over and over again. He also said that I was not to interfere—with what I'm not sure, but perhaps Hermes can enlighten us here."

"Whoever gave this cure to Quinn Sondheim is *not* from the Ochrana; he may have in fact disguised himself as one of my people to fool him, as a matter of fact. Or perhaps he chose to appear as a human; I am not sure of that. But this I am sure of; my mission was to come to Earth because my people are desperate to know where the Feindliche are receiving their supply chains to build weapons and space crafts. The intelligence that I was able to collect so far pointed me towards Sondheim Incorporated. I was about to travel inside of Sondheim Incorporated in this metropolis when this man stopped me," Hermes reported and pointed to McGregor. "The Ochrana and the Feindliche are unfortunately at war . . . we have been desperately battling one another for the past solar year."

"Walking into a major corporation like that with a giant gun isn't exactly the best approach," McGregor stated matter-of-factly. "I wouldn't have seen him except for the fact that my magnafone somehow managed to track his cloaking field."

"What kind of gun?" Armstrong inquired.

Hermes motioned to the huge gun that sat behind the padded bench beside him. This projectile was nothing like anything that Armstrong had seen before. Its barrel was nearly three and a half feet long and steel blue. There was no actual trigger to the device that he could see, but it did closely resemble the structure of a military Remington model 700 also minus the scope.

"Well, that'll definitely stand out in a fight. Sniper rifle?" the ex-cop asked.

"It is called the Y'Skoda and fires much like a hybrid electro-thermal light gas gun. It does not use projectiles encased with gunpowder."

"Um . . . we don't have anything like that yet. What's the size of the clip?"

Hermes touched his talons right beneath his ear and blinked hard a few times as his translator interpreted the question for him. "There is no clip. As I stated, it fires like a hybrid electro-thermal—"

"Never mind about that, then. So if you're from the Ochrana and your enemy is the Feindliche, then do you know who represents them?"

"I do. A member of the Feindliche's special infiltration team has deceived Quinn Sondheim. His alias is Mercury, and he was delegated to use any means necessary to retrieve these materials . . . rare earths, as you call them. Of course, that is likely not his real name."

"But why? I mean, I understand that your two species are at war, but what do the Feindliche hope to accomplish out of all this?" Armstrong demanded.

"They are trying to strike the Ochrana as hard as they possibly can with the modus operandi of complete and total annihilation, much like the same strategy that . . ." Hermes touched the skin beneath his ear again. "That the German dictator Adolf Hitler used during World War II in the last century on your world. He did not use diplomacy, and neither did they."

"What started all this? How long has this war been going on?" McGregor spoke up and drank from his brandy.

"I do not know that, but I can assure you that the Feindliche are growing stronger by the day. The only way that we the Ochrana can defend ourselves now is to break the supply chain, which is why you found me where you did."

"We should try to contact Quinn himself; he's an altruistic person and would likely try to shut everything down," Liszt suggested.

"What if that fails? What if these brain washed people are just loyal to those bad aliens . . . uh . . . the . . . the . . . Feind-whatevers and not Quinn himself?" Armstrong shot back.

"Feindliche," Hermes corrected him.

"It's a chance that we'll have to take, then," McGregor responded neutrally. "Ms. Liszt, will it be a problem with you to eliminate Wooster? That'll give us total access to Sondheim without any issues."

"Before I agree to do anything here, you need to be more forthright with us," Liszt ordered and pointed her index finger at him. "You need our help, and none of us appreciate being misled like this."

"Armstrong, I'm going to need you for this assault that we'll be making on Sondheim Incorporated. I still want to go through with this."

Nestor silently crossed his arms and shook his head 'no'.

"Is it normal for human beings to distrust one another like this? You said that he was your subordinate and would obey any command that you gave him," Hermes directed his question towards McGregor. "That does not seem to be the case here."

"That's because he's a security consultant and not a soldier," Liszt replied coldly. "Hypothetically speaking, Nestor can still walk away from his job and not suffer any consequences, whereas a soldier most definitely would."

She did it again. She called me by my first name. I hope that McGregor didn't notice that.

"Yet there were some for you," Hermes noted. "McGregor told me."

"I didn't exactly leave quietly or give Wooster two weeks' notice. I uploaded a harmful but temporary virus into my former company's security systems and shot my way out of the complex. Now, before this gets out of control here, McGregor, you need to come clean with the both of us. In fact, it would probably be to your advantage to be honest with Hermes as well, since he appears to be a potential ally." She crossed her arms over her chest.

"I noticed that you haven't touched your beverage, Hermes," McGregor said and motioned his head towards the water.

"I cannot consume it without a proper treatment. I did not bring the means to do so when I traveled to your planet," the alien replied. "You should answer Liszt and Armstrong's concerns."

"What do you think?"

"I have not had enough time with you to develop a true opinion. However, the longer you resist sharing the truth with your fellow species, the less likely I am to trust you, McGregor. I also do not require my gun to inflict pain upon your frail body. As a matter of fact, I see no fewer than twelve different ways to do so in this mode of transportation." Hermes' two pairs of eyes swept throughout the cabin.

That's impressive, Armstrong noted. *I only could count five myself.*

McGregor finished the rest of his brandy and put the snifter down onto the bar. "Then it appears that our game of chess is at a stalemate." He took a deep breath and sat down onto a stool next to Armstrong. "Long ago, I worked for the government contractor and research company named Lochsummit Miller. An experiment went *very* wrong there; it was to test the nano technology that makes up the suit that you yourself wear, Armstrong. More than one person died, if not several in the process."

"I thought that Nathan Falk was the one who crafted that suit," Armstrong finally spoke up. "And speaking of which, he should make it more fireproof."

"Then that would explain how he made it a helluva lot lighter. But going back to my story here, I left the company when they wouldn't do anything about these incidents. They insisted that we press on through it all."

Liszt leaned against the wall. "So why start a company that specializes in medical technology and pharmacology?"

"The original purpose of Zionastra was to be a U.S. government contractor, but then as time went on, I saw that medical and pharmaceutical technology would be far more fruitful than developing weapons. There are always conflicts going on in between nations, but there are far more diseases that are trying to conquer us all. Cancer doesn't care what color your skin is nor whom you call your god."

"Is that how your wars start on Earth?" Hermes wondered.

"Not all of them, no," Liszt disagreed. "But let's get back to the point here. Sondheim also worked for Lochsummit Miller. Did the two of you know one another or work together?"

"He was there, yes, but he worked in a different department."

Armstrong's lips pursed themselves firmly against one another. He took a large complete breath from his nose before he spoke. "I'm only going to ask you this one more time, sir. *Why* do you want this technology?"

"I apologize, but I must report to my superiors soon," Hermes interrupted them all. "Also, we must hurry and get in touch with Quinn Sondheim. The sooner we can talk to him and impart this knowledge to him, the better off we might all be."

"Hold on," Armstrong said and stood. "I'd like to know what your *real* name is, and why you assumed the name of a man who died over seventy years ago."

"I assumed the name McGregor when I left Lochsummit Miller; it was for my own protection from them as well as . . . well—"

"The authorities, perhaps?" Liszt chimed in.

McGregor shrugged. "Look, have either of you considered the situation from my standpoint? Neither of you can truly appreciate what kind of sacrifices I have made for the good of my company or even humanity at this point."

"That remains to be seen. We're not making unreasonable requests here."

"You have no choice but to trust me in order to keep your present resources." He pulled out his magnafone from his pocket. "I have but to draw my fingers across this screen here a few times to deactivate your company credit lines and your fancy electronics, Armstrong."

"That sounds like a threat to me," Liszt's eyes narrowed as she said this.

"Jumping to conclusions again, Ms. Liszt?" McGregor glanced at her. "Or are you taking sides with my employee here because you might feel lost and have no direction?"

Armstrong's breath almost hitched at that last question. He almost thought that McGregor had picked up on her subtle change in attitude towards himself; thankfully, he hadn't done so yet.

"There is no arguing with pretenders who claim to have divine knowledge and a divine mission. They are possessed with the sin of pride. McGregor has not made that claim, while Quinn Sondheim nearly has. I have seen photographs depicting him as practically the savior of the human race all over the internet and something you call television here, yet all he did was to accept someone else's brilliant scientific work. Some of your kind even dares to call it a miracle. You must make a choice here, Armstrong; your decision alone will make or break the path that we will forge together or separately from here," Hermes wisely told him.

The ex-cop's head sunk into his hand. "Then what would you do?"

"That is irrelevant; your superior has asked you where you stand."

Another minute of silence passed as Armstrong poured over every scenario that he possibly could in his head. None of them ended well unless he picked his least favorite option, which was to trust McGregor for now. He sighed and made eye contact with his employer. "All right. I'll play it your way, Boss."

"Good choice, Armstrong," McGregor said and nodded with approval.

I hope I don't regret it later on.

Nestor's eyes traveled over to Liszt's. Her stoicism made it once again nearly impossible for him to read her facial expressions and body language. After McGregor turned his back, though, she raised a cautious eyebrow towards him.

The alien arose from his chair and reactivated his holographic disguise. "I must contact my home planet. Excuse my absence."

Liszt touched Armstrong by the arm. "We should talk. I'll meet you upstairs on the observation deck." Seconds later, she also disappeared as she made her way up the stairs.

Armstrong's eyes swept over the alien weapon with amusement, then suddenly remembered that he had to be somewhere else. "I'll be back in a minute, Boss," the ex-cop stated and followed her.

He climbed both sets of stairs and found Liszt leaning against the rail on the top deck. She was facing the bow of the yacht and spun around when she heard his footsteps on the metallic ladder. "Did McGregor send you up here, or are you present because I asked to speak with you?" she asked.

"I'm here because you wanted to talk; what he wants isn't my problem."

"Oh, but it is. You're still his employee."

He rolled his eyes. "Did you ask me to come up here just so that you could ridicule me privately because of what I said back there, or—"

She gave him a smirk. "Relax, Tiger. Trusting McGregor for now is a good idea. Don't forget about my little cache." Liszt then removed her magnafone from her shorts' back pocket. "This conversation may also prove to give us some leverage later on, just in case he decides to be . . . mmm . . . uncooperative."

He glanced downward at the magnafone and took a step towards her. "So when did you hit record?" he whispered.

"When we came onboard, of course," she answered him back with the same volume.

"Good thinking, Dirty Harriet." Armstrong gave her a grin and returned the conversation back to its previous decibel level. "So, I'll plan to infiltrate Sondheim Incorporated here with Hermes and McGregor. What uh . . . what do you plan to do?"

"Just what McGregor asked me to do, "she said with a shrug. "He wanted me to go after Wooster and remove him from the equation permanently."

His eyes narrowed. "You're not going to—"

"Kill him?" She waved a hand dismissively at his remark. "No. But I'll take him professionally out of the picture and do that however I can."

"Can I ask . . . how you intend to do that?"

"Curiosity can be deadly, Tiger. Do you like puzzles?"

"Only if they wear perfume."

They were about two feet apart now, and she gave him full eye contact after his latest retort. "You've been thinking about something that happened earlier in the day to us, haven't you?"

"I can't say that it didn't cross my mind. I also get the impression, however, that you might have done the same thing at least once," Armstrong returned civilly.

"It has, but . . .—"

"I'm not asking for marriage or a lifetime commitment here. Maybe you'd like to . . . test out the waters is all . . . take a dive, maybe?"

"I need some time, Nestor." She folded her arms over her chest.

He nodded. "I can live with that. Rome wasn't conquered in one day."

The corners of Liszt's mouths gradually perked up. "Indeed. Neither was the ancient city of Troy." She paused to think for a moment, then went on. "What kind of combat skills do you think that McGregor's got?"

"I have no idea. I hope that he's the tactical sort that will just let me and Hermes handle the assault, but anything's possible. Will you be all right with Wooster?"

"Of course. He's made advances on me before, so that card is already in the hand that I've been dealt, so to speak."

"Great." Armstrong's jaw tensed.

She noticed his discomfort and placed a hand onto his arm. "It'll be child's play, honestly, Tiger. Besides, if I get over my head, there's always Leontine." Liszt patted her shoulder holster.

"Just . . . be careful, all right?"

"Only if you do the same for me."

"Okay." He cleared his throat and turned his back. "Need me to drop you off at the airport?"

"Let's stay at our hotel for the evening, and then I'll depart in the morning for California. Sound good to you?"

"Yeah. I'll uh . . . give you a buzz when we finish this meeting." Armstrong went down the ladder and journeyed back down to McGregor.

After he traveled back down the stairs from the navigational deck, McGregor turned towards him. "Has my niece made it to my townhouse?"

"I haven't spoken with Falk yet," Armstrong told him. "I can't tell you the truth because I honestly don't know. We made plans almost immediately after you contacted me this morning to get here."

"So, have you managed to procure Ms. Liszt's trust yet? Will she be amenable to our plans?" McGregor poured himself another snifter of brandy.

"She'll play ball with me."

"Use whatever means are necessary to do so, Armstrong. I have found her to be useful to our cause."

"Could you clarify that, please, sir?" Armstrong's eyes narrowed as he tried to read his employer's nearly stoic expressions.

"I don't believe that it's necessary to do so; use your best judgment. Just don't break the law. I'd like a few minutes of privacy now, Mr. Armstrong." McGregor lifted a hand slightly upward to dismiss his subordinate.

Did he just order me to seduce Penelope? What the hell does this guy want? Why didn't he tell me more about what happened at Lochsummit Miller? And why do I feel even more confused now than when I got here?

"Yes, sir, but before I go, could I have that drink first, please?"

McGregor laughed and unscrewed the cap from a bottle of Tanqueray gin. "Dirty gin martini, no ice, two olives?"

"Yes, sir, if you would."

"My pleasure, Armstrong." The tycoon began to make the drink with a wide smile. "If you'd be so good as to let

Hermes know that we'll reconvene here in the morning, I would be most grateful."

"Will do, sir." About a minute later, McGregor handed his employee his preferred beverage of choice in its proper glass. As the ex-cop left, he glanced over his shoulder to watch McGregor warm his brandy by swirling it around continuously in the snifter.

to be continued . . .